The Three Fat Men

A Fairytale

Yuri Olesha

Translated by Hugh Aplin

Modern Voices

Modern Voices
Published by Hesperus Press Limited
19 Bulstrode Street, London W1U 2JN
www.hesperuspress.com

First published in Russian in 1928
First published by Hesperus Press Limited, 2011

Introduction and English language translation © Hugh Aplin, 2011
Foreword © Graeme Garden, 2011

Юрий Олеша «Три толстяка»
Russian text copyright © 2011 by Varvara Shklovskaya-Kordi
Translation rights into the English language are granted by FTM Agency, Ltd.,
Russia, 2011 © English translation rights, 2011

Designed and typeset by Fraser Muggeridge studio
Printed in Jordan by Jordan National Press

ISBN: 978-1-84391-452-5

Contents

Foreword

The Three Fat Men is a funny book, both 'ha-ha' and 'peculiar'. Described by the author as a 'fairy tale' (although there are no fairies or other supernatural creatures in evidence) it is a satirical allegory in which a cavalcade of colourful characters becomes embroiled in revolutionary upheaval, their predicaments and their resolutions becoming increasingly bizarre.

The book is beautifully written and imaginatively translated, a fantastical story observed with detachment and delivered in a cool voice. The writing is rich and decorative rather than ornamental, graced with deft little touches that brighten the effect. Even the simplest of descriptive passages can be invested with Olesha's lyrical magic:

> The doctor covered his ears with his collar and presented his back to the wind. Then the wind started on the stars. First it would blow them out, then roll them around, and then knock them down behind the black triangles of roofs. When it was tired of that game, it thought of the clouds. But the clouds collapsed like towers. All at once at that point the wind became cold: it turned cold out of spite.

Olesha was rightly proud of his way with a metaphor, and the frequent similes scattered throughout the book are always perfectly chosen yet fresh and unexpected. For example:

> Beneath his eye, one of them had a dark bruise in the shape of an unattractive rose or of an attractive frog.

Or:

> Old Augustus had shut his eyes and, terror-stricken, was

rocking about like a Chinese emperor trying to decide whether to cut off the criminal's head or to make him eat a live rat without sugar.

It's the lack of sugar on the rat that elevates the comparison to high comicality. Elsewhere he describes a dancing class, conducted by the splendidly named dancing master, 'Onetwothreesir':

> Couples were spinning around. There were so many of them and they were sweating so, you might have thought that some motley and vile-tasting soup was on the boil.
>
> Spinning around in the general hurly-burly, first a gentleman, then a lady would start to resemble either a long-tailed turnip, or a cabbage leaf, or something else unrecognisable, coloured and peculiar that might be found in a bowl of soup.
>
> And in this bowl of soup, Onetwothreesir performed the duties of the spoon, and rightly so, as he was very tall, slender and curved.

And a rather less light-hearted example:

> The running people were approaching the town. Whole heaps of people were falling along the way. It was as if multicoloured rags were being scattered onto the greenery.

Yes, this is the description, in the first chapter, of the massacre of workers by mounted guards. There are real weapons in this story and people are killed. The depiction of such violence might appear shocking in a work for children, though perhaps no more shocking than the horrors depicted by the Brothers Grimm, or those seen in today's computer games. And we should remember that when *The Three Fat Men* was first published in 1928, a child of ten would have grown up in post-revolutionary Russia, and lived through the bitter civil war. Such brutal events would have been almost commonplace to them, while in the USA kids were enjoying *Steamboat Willie*, Mickey Mouse's first sound movie.

As a work of satirical fantasy, *The Three Fat Men* has often been compared with Lewis Carroll's *Alice's Adventures in Wonderland*, and the works are indeed comparable, if only because they are so utterly different.

Alice is a work of surrealism, taking place in a dream world in which things just 'are' with no explanation (for instance we are never told who or what made the 'Eat Me/Drink Me' cake and potion). The creatures and events follow a kind of lateral and somewhat sinister logic which as a child I always found disturbing. And Alice's adventures are domestic satire, carica-turing figures familiar to the author and to the real Alice. Olesha's book is a political satire on a much grander scale, and, to my mind at least, much funnier.

The Three Fat Men sits more comfortably in the realm of magic realism, in which the cause and effect laws of physics and logic are more or less intact, but irrational twists spring out from time to time to surprise us. In one delicious sequence, the Balloon Seller is blown, with his balloons, into the palace kitchens and lands in a giant cake. The cooks, deciding the cake is irreparable, leave the Balloon Seller stuck in it, decorate him a bit, then wheel him into the dining room. Before the Fat Men and their fat guests can cut off his head to get at the goodies they assume to be inside, the Balloon Seller manages to escape through a bottomless saucepan.

Writing visual comedy or physical slapstick for the stage or screen is a curious business. Broadly speaking a visual joke is funny twice – once when it springs into the mind of the writer, and once again when an audience laughs at it. Between those two moments it is an act of faith. On the page it is generally a series of careful instructions as to how the effect may be achieved, and the comedy is not necessarily present in the words. Visual comedy on the printed page is a different matter. The reader must be able to laugh at the description itself, and this is where Olesha excels, his detailed accounts of physical events conjuring up such vivid pictures that it is impossible not to respond to them. The book is full of comic visual gems, from the Zoologist falling through a tree to the quill pen flung like a dart into the backside of a guard, or here where Prospero the armourer and Suok the girl dancer are ransacking the kitchen in search of the bottomless saucepan:

> This was the demolition of the glittering glass, copper, hot, sweet, fragrant world of the confectionary. The armourer was searching for the most important saucepan. Inside it was his salvation and the salvation of his little saviour.
>
> He was overturning jars, throwing frying-pans, funnels, plates and dishes around. Glass was flying in all directions and breaking with a ringing and a crashing; there was a twisting column of spilled flour like a simoom in the Sahara; there rose a whirlwind of almonds, currants, cherries; granulated sugar streamed from the shelves with the din of a waterfall; a flood of syrup rose to a depth of a whole foot; water splashed, fruits rolled around, copper towers of saucepans collapsed. Everything was upside down. It's like that when you're asleep sometimes, when you're having a dream and you know that it's a dream, and so you can do whatever you want.

Olesha's satire is generalised – he doesn't spell out in grim detail specifically why or how the Three Fat Men (who respectively own all the grain, coal and iron) are cruel and oppressive. Their chief sin seems to be their weight, and fatness is the feature that distinguishes the rich from the poor. When alarmed, the Three Fat Men begin to grow fatter, collars and buttons bursting under the strain. When the workers revolt, the Palace Guards split into two factions, for and against the Three Fat Men, like the Red and White Cossacks in the civil war that followed the Russian Revolution.

The Circus is a central element in the story, and the book itself has the feel of a narrative circus act, or perhaps a pantomime. The cast of gloriously eccentric characters includes the bewildered Dr Gaspar; the rebel leaders, armourer Prospero and gymnast Tibullus; Suok the girl dancer; and Tutti the boy who is raised by the Three Fat Men to be their heir, but despite being trained to be heartless and cruel prefers to play with his beloved lifelike doll. Whether any of these can be supposed to represent the real historical figures involved in the revolution needs a better political historian than me to deduce.

Judging by this book, we might assume that Olesha's simple, uncritical and possibly naive view of the Russian Revolution left him unprepared for the brutality of Stalinism. The bright future he envisages after the overthrow of the Three Fat Men does not include a Five Year Plan leading to mass industrialisation, collective farming, chaos and famine and the death of millions. So it is no surprise that Olesha lost faith and fell out of favour with the Soviet authorities. In the 1930s, he was condemned by the literary establishment, and, fearing arrest, he stopped creating anything of literary value. If he had been bold (or foolish) enough to carry on writing his child-friendly satirical allegories, who knows what he might have come up with? He might even have written *Animal Farm*.

The Three Fat Men is that rare thing, an intelligent and funny children's book that will appeal to children as well as adults.

– Graeme Garden, 2011

Introduction

The Three Fat Men is one of the unquestioned classics of Soviet children's literature, alongside the poems of Samuil Marshak and Kornei Chukovsky, the plays of Yevgeny Shvarts and the prose of Alexander Grin. It is unusual, though, for the fact that Yuri Olesha deals explicitly in this, his 'fairytale', with the theme of revolution; and he wrote later of his aim thereby to 'revolutionise the fairytale'. This might have seemed certain to ensure his work a secure place, both immediate and long-term, in the Soviet canon. However, the book's biography is not quite so straightforward. One explanation for this may lie in Olesha's very definition of his genre as 'fairytale': how could the proletariat's titanic struggle against oppression be squeezed into the confines of a work of, in large part, comic fantasy? And were the tale's heroes and heroine fitting standard-bearers for Bolshevik ideals? Moreover, was the style of Olesha's writing itself a suitable vehicle for the expression of righteous indignation about the exploitation of the masses?

The question of the book's audience can look somewhat problematic too. Although it is certainly enjoyed by children from quite an early age, there are aspects of the story that are scarcely typical of a work intended for very young readers. It is symptomatic that the English version by Fainna Glagoleva, regularly reprinted in the latter decades of the last century by the Soviet Union's specialist foreign-language publishing house, Progress, omits a considerable number of words, phrases, and even complete sentences from the Russian original, becoming as a result more a sanitised paraphrase than a faithful translation. Telling, too, is the fact that the edition of Olesha's works from which the present translation was made is completed by the writer's acknowledged masterpiece, the novel *Envy*, his reminiscences of leading literary figures of his time, and extracts from his notebooks on the topic of writing – hardly the stuff of a volume for children.

Olesha was, in fact, never primarily a children's writer, and it is thus somewhat ironic that by far his greatest popular success came with this, his one book written with that readership in mind.

Yuri Karlovich Olesha was born in 1899 into a family of Polish gentry of modest means, which moved to the cosmopolitan port of Odessa in 1902. There Olesha studied first at grammar school, and subsequently in the law faculty of the Imperial Novorossiya University; more importantly though, he also became involved as a teenager in Odessa's thriving literary scene. He wrote and published poetry, and made the acquaintance of many of the talented young writers then living there, among whom were Isaac Babel, Valentin Katayev, Eduard Bagritsky and the future satirical team of (Ilya) Ilf and (Yevgeny) Petrov.

Olesha was active during the Civil War on the side of the Bolsheviks, and in 1921, while his parents immigrated to Poland, he himself moved to Kharkov, where he worked as a journalist and propagandist. A year later he settled in Moscow and found employment writing satirical verse and articles for the railwaymen's newspaper *The Siren*, which numbered among its regular contributors many of his old friends from Odessa, as well as Mikhail Bulgakov.

The fairytale *The Three Fat Men* was Olesha's first lengthy work in prose, and was written in 1924. Eleven years later, when a ballet based on the book was in preparation at the Bolshoi Theatre, the author wrote in the programme notes:

Working on *The Three Fat Men*, I was paying tribute to the talents which seem to me the most striking there can possibly be in the sphere of art. Those are the talents of the men who can invent fairytales. A fairytale is a reflection of grandiose phenomena in the life of society. And the men who can turn a complex social process into a gentle and transparent form are for me the most amazing poets. I consider the Brothers Grimm, Perrault, Andersen, Hauff and Hoffmann to be such poets.

Given these Western European models, it is no wonder that the world Olesha created in *The Three Fat Men* has little to link it with Russia – other than its revolution. The names of the characters are primarily, albeit not exclusively, Italianate, and the general atmosphere of the setting is, due in part to that eclectic mix of names, geographically non-specific; chronologically it is pre-twentieth century (carriages, cavalrymen and so forth), but otherwise unfixed. The environment that is perhaps the key to the timeless and ubiquitous qualities of the text is that of the circus – a long-established mode of entertainment, free from geographical boundaries. It would not be outlandish to describe the book as a narrative of revolution as circus performance, with a large number of the key scenes being played out in front of various different audiences. It has been suggested, indeed, that *The Three Fat Men* is one of the best examples in Russian literature of what the eminent critic Mikhail Bakhtin termed 'carnival': such elements as crowd involvement, the violation of customary natural laws (identified by Olesha as vital to the magic of the acrobat) and buffoonery all typify the circus, and run through the book as well, contributing to the subversion of the established order that is characteristic of carnival.

Certainly the circus was an art form that Olesha held dear: an enthusiast in childhood, he wrote a sketch entitled 'At the Circus' in 1929, and returned to the topic in another sketch, 'Spectacles', in 1937. Dominant in these pieces is the figure of the tightrope walker, whose appearance is described as 'fairy-tale': 'He has a demonic face with a protruding chin and a long nose. His eyes flash […] he wears a black and yellow leotard, he is Harlequin, his leg looks like a snake'; and similarly: 'We sense the fragrance of fairytale when we see the acrobat performing a somersault. The acrobat is undoubtedly the most fantastic figure of the circus.' It is hardly surprising, then, that one of the heroes of *The Three Fat Men* is an acrobat, as is the heroine.

Not only did Olesha admire the acrobats of the circuses of his childhood, he also confesses in his memoirs, *Not a Day without a Line*, that even the object of his first love was an acrobat, ostensibly female, but who subsequently proved to be a boy. The heroine of Olesha's fairytale can be linked with the writer's love life more closely still, however, as her name, Suok, was the maiden name of his wife, Olga, to whom the book was dedicated, and her younger sister, Serafima, with whom Olesha lived for some time before his marriage, until she left him for the poet who would eventually become the book's publisher, Vladimir Narbut. The figure of the fearless little dancer was readily recognisable to contemporaries as Serafima, and it is easy to see similarities between her husband and the fearsomely powerful Prospero, another hero who, like the acrobat, has certain demonic associations.

Nonetheless, if *The Three Fat Men* can begin to seem like a rather sinister reworking of some of the circumstances of its creator's life, the closing paragraph of 'At the Circus' explains the inevitable lightening of the mood of Olesha's circus world: 'We're in favour of sport at the circus, in favour of humour! We don't want to be horrified at the circus. We're not interested in seeing an actor killed, falling from a trapeze.' And the lightening is achieved, of course, through humour, just as the thrills of a circus performance are interspersed – or sometimes combined – with the fooling of the clowns. At times Olesha even resorts to clown-like slapstick, as in the scene where the acrobat is pursued by three fairground performers, grotesque parodies of the tale's three heroes.

Often amusing, too, are the examples of Olesha's most striking literary tool, which are very much in evidence here: in *Not a Day without a Line* the writer represented himself as opening a metaphor shop, which he hoped would make him rich, and in a series of entertaining pages he went on to provide ample proof of his mastery of this figure of speech. A reason for his frequent deployment of it in a work for children is also suggested in the same passage, when he writes:

What I know for sure about myself is that I have a gift for naming things in a new way. Sometimes more successfully, sometimes less so. The purpose of this gift I don't know. For some reason people need it. On hearing a metaphor – even in passing, even only just catching it – a child emerges from play for a moment, listens, and then laughs approvingly. And so it is needed.

The images throughout the pages of this book are unquestionably enough to make any reader pause and take note. The often outrageous similes which embellish Olesha's otherwise spare prose are such that, in Russian literature, perhaps only Nikolai Gogol's could successfully compete with them. Indeed, Gogol is arguably one of Olesha's most significant influences, and another writer commonly associated with carnival.

Although completed in 1924, *The Three Fat Men* appeared in print only in 1928, after the successful publication of *Envy* a year earlier. It can be conjectured that the idea of publishing a book by a virtually unknown young writer, who had dealt with the theme of revolution using a genre dependent on fantasy and the taste of children, was simply too whimsical for the publishers of the mid-1920s. The subsequent 'serious' novel of contemporary life cleared the path. Neither, however, met with universal approval. It is scarcely surprising that *Envy* provoked a mixed critical reaction: its examination of the consequences of the establishment of Bolshevik power for the spiritual life of the individual within the new collective is at the very least ambiguous. But the fairytale too, despite dealing in an ideologically positive way with the overthrow of a tyrannical regime, received its share of criticism. 'How Stories for Children Should Not Be' was the title of one response, which highlighted what was perceived as a sugar-coated treatment of revolution; 'the children of the Land of the Soviets will find here no call to struggle, to labour, no heroic example' a critic railed; it was accused of being essentially 'cold', with its author too much concerned with the world of objects, to the detriment of the exploration of characters' emotions. It was suggested that the heroism of the revolt against the eponymous despots was lost in a welter of descriptive detail. Much of the criticism seems to have forgotten the fact that the book was intended for children, who are likely to be at least as interested in details of a heroine's dress as in the pathos of her readiness for self-sacrifice in the advancement of the revolutionary cause. Yet the book did find a staunch and still influential defender in Anatoly Lunacharsky, the former People's Commissar for Enlightenment, who saw in it 'a heartfelt apologia for the artistic intelligentsia accepting the revolution': it is, indeed, tempting to see Dr Gaspar Arneri as a fellow-traveller – a specialist prepared to lend his skills to the furtherance of the just revolutionary aspirations of the working class to which he clearly does not himself belong.

If the publication of *Envy* and *The Three Fat Men* at the end of the 1920s seemed to betoken a flourishing career for their author, with the onset of the 1930s his initial success was to prove short-lived. Olesha adapted *Envy* as a play entitled *A Conspiracy of Feelings* in 1929, but it was soon banned; rehearsals of another play, *A List of Good Deeds* (1930), were begun under the outstanding director Vsevolod Meyerhold, but it too was banned. Olesha, like his old friend Isaac Babel, attended the Soviet Writers' Congress of 1934, at which the supremacy of the Socialist Realist method was proclaimed. Babel's speech famously asserted his mastery of the genre of silence; Olesha in part apologised for his work, and in part expressed his intention to write in a manner more fitting for the age. The requirements of Socialist Realism could not, however, accommodate Olesha's talents, and criticism of him and his writing grew, until, like many others of his generation, he found himself forced into Babel's genre. He died in 1960, in straitened circumstances, but with his wit and humour intact: upon learning that he had earned the right to the highest category of funeral for a writer, he apparently asked if he could be relegated to a lower one and given the difference in cost in cash, while he was still alive to enjoy it.

Olesha's abiding success remained *The Three Fat Men*: as well as the ballet of 1935, it has inspired opera, film and theatrical adaptations, and has delighted Russian children of every generation since the 1920s. But one of the great Russian poets of the twentieth century, Osip Mandelstam, recognised its value beyond the children's bookshelf too. In 'The Duchess's Fan', a review of contemporary literature dating from 1929, he accorded the fairytale the highest praise:

If Olesha's *Fat Men* were a translated book, any attentive reader would say: how strange that I never knew this remarkable foreign author until now. He must be considered a classic in his homeland, thank goodness that, albeit late, he *has* been translated. [...] This is crystal-clear prose, suffused through and through with the fire of revolution, a book of European scale.

– Hugh Aplin, 2011

The Three Fat Men

Part One
Tibullus
the Tightrope Walker

Dr Gaspar Arneri's Hectic Day

The time of wizards is over. And most probably there never were any really. That's all just inventions and fairytales for very small children. Quite simply, some tricksters used to be so skilled at deceiving all sorts of idle folk that those tricksters were taken for sorcerers and wizards.

There was once a doctor like that. His name was Gaspar Arneri. A naive person, a fairground loafer, a half-educated student might have taken him for a wizard too. This doctor did indeed do such amazing things that they really did seem like miracles. Of course, he had nothing in common with the wizards and charlatans who used to dupe excessively trusting people.

Dr Gaspar Arneri was a scholar. He had studied maybe a hundred branches of learning. In any event, there was no one in the country wiser or more learned than Gaspar Arneri.

Everybody knew of his scholarship – the miller, the soldier, grand ladies and ministers. And schoolchildren sang a song about him with the following chorus:

> *How to catch a fox by the tail,*
> *How to fly from earth to a star,*
> *How to make hot steam from a stone –*
> *All is known by Dr Gaspar.*

One summer's day, in June, when some very fine weather had come along, Dr Gaspar Arneri decided to set out on a long walk to collect certain sorts of herbs and beetles.

Dr Gaspar was not a young man, and so was apprehensive about rain and wind. Leaving the house, he would wind a thick scarf about his neck, put on glasses for protection against dust, take a walking stick so as not to stumble, and would in general take great precautions when preparing for a walk.

On this occasion the day was wonderful: the sun did nothing but shine; the grass was so green that it even produced a sensation of sweetness in your mouth; dandelions flew, birds chirped; a light breeze blew about like a flimsy ball-gown.

'Now, that's good,' said the doctor, 'only I must take my cape all the same, because the summer weather's deceptive. It might rain.'

The doctor saw to his domestic affairs, blew on his glasses, picked up his little green leather case, like a valise, and off he went.

The most interesting places were outside of town, where the Palace of the Three Fat Men was. The doctor visited those places most frequently of all. The Palace of the Three Fat Men stood in the midst of an enormous park. The park was surrounded by deep canals. Over the canals hung black, iron bridges. The bridges were defended by the palace guard – guardsmen in black oilskin hats with yellow plumes. Right up to the skyline around the park there were meadows strewn with flowers, there were groves and ponds. This was an excellent place for walks. This was where the most interesting species of herbs grew, where the most beautiful beetles buzzed and where the most artful birds sang.

'But it's a long way to go on foot. I'll walk as far as the town wall and then hire a cab to take me to the palace park,' thought the doctor.

There were more people than usual beside the town wall.

'Is it Sunday today?' the doctor thought doubtfully. 'I don't think so. Today's Tuesday.'

The doctor went closer.

The whole square was awash with people. The doctor saw artisans in grey cloth jackets with green cuffs; sailors with faces the colour of clay; well-to-do burghers in coloured waistcoats with their wives, whose skirts were like rose bushes; traders with their carafes, trays, ice-cream makers and braziers; skinny street

6

actors, green, yellow and multi-coloured, as though made from a patchwork quilt; tiny little children pulling jolly ginger dogs by their tails.

Everyone was jostling in front of the town gates. The huge iron gates, as high as a house, were shut tight.

'Why are the gates closed?' the doctor wondered in surprise.

The crowd was noisy, everybody was talking loudly, shouting and quarrelling, but no real sense could be made of anything.

The doctor went up to a young woman holding a fat, grey cat on her arm and asked:

'Would you be so kind as to explain what's going on here? Why are there so many people, what's the reason for their excitement and why are the town gates closed?'

'The guardsmen aren't letting people out of the town...'

'And why not?'

'So that they don't help those who've already left the town and gone off towards the Palace of the Three Fat Men...'

'I don't understand a thing, Citizen, and beg you to forgive me...'

'Oh dear, do you really not know that Prospero the armourer and Tibullus the acrobat have led the people to take the Palace of the Three Fat Men by storm today?'

'Prospero the armourer?...'

'Yes, Citizen... The wall's high, and the palace guard's marksmen have taken up positions on the other side. No one can leave the town, and the palace guard will slaughter those who went with Prospero the armourer.'

And indeed, several very distant shots did crash out.

The woman dropped the fat cat. The cat fell with a plop, like unbaked dough. The crowd began bellowing.

'So I've missed such a significant event,' thought the doctor. 'True, I haven't left my room for a whole month. I've been working behind closed doors. I didn't know anything...'

At that moment, even further away, there were several bangs from a cannon. The thunder began bouncing like a ball, and rolled away on the wind. It wasn't only the doctor who took fright and hurriedly retreated several paces – the whole crowd shied away and split apart. The children burst into tears; the doves scattered, with their wings crackling; the dogs cowered and started howling.

Heavy cannon fire started up. An unimaginable noise arose. The crowd pressed up against the gates and cried,

'Prospero! Prospero!'

'Down with the Three Fat Men!'

Dr Gaspar completely lost his head. He was recognised in the crowd because a lot of people knew him to look at. Some rushed towards him as though seeking his protection. But the doctor himself was almost crying.

'What's happening out there? How can we find out what's happening there, outside the gates? Perhaps the people are winning; but perhaps everyone's already been shot down!'

Then ten or so men ran off to where three narrow little streets started out from the square. On the corner was a house with a tall old tower. The doctor, along with the others, decided to clamber up into the tower. Downstairs was a laundry like a bath-house. It was as dark as in a cellar there. A spiral staircase led upwards. Light penetrated through small, narrow windows, but there was very little of it, and everyone ascended slowly, with great difficulty, all the more as the staircase was ramshackle and had a broken handrail. It isn't hard to imagine how much effort and anxiety it cost Dr Gaspar to ascend to the very top floor. In any event, as early as the twentieth step his cry rang out in the darkness,

'Oh dear, my heart's bursting and I've lost a heel!'

The doctor had lost his cape while still in the square, after the tenth cannon shot.

At the top of the tower there was a platform surrounded by a stone parapet. From there a view opened up for at least some fifty kilometres around. There was no time to admire the view, though that was what the view deserved. Everyone looked towards where the battle was taking place.

'I have a pair of binoculars. I always carry eight-lens binoculars with me. Here they are,' said the doctor, and undid the strap.

The binoculars passed from hand to hand.

Dr Gaspar saw a host of people on a green expanse. They were running towards the town. They were fleeing. From a distance the people seemed like little multi-coloured flags. Guardsmen were chasing after the people on horseback.

Dr Gaspar thought it was all like a magic lantern picture. The sun was shining brightly, the greenery was gleaming. Bombs were exploding like bits of cotton wool, and a flame would appear for a second, as if someone were directing reflections of sunrays into the crowd. Horses were prancing, rearing up and spinning like tops. The park and the Palace of the Three Fat Men were clouded with white, transparent smoke.

'They're running away... The people are defeated!'

The running people were approaching the town. Whole heaps of people were falling along the way. It was as if multi-coloured rags were being scattered onto the greenery.

A bomb whistled over the square.

Someone took fright and dropped the binoculars. The bomb exploded, and everyone who was at the top of the tower rushed back down inside the tower.

A metal worker got his leather apron caught on some sort of hook. He looked round, saw something terrible, and started yelling for the whole square to hear:

'Run! They've captured Prospero the armourer! They'll be entering the town at any moment!'

Hubbub started up in the square. The crowd flooded back from the gates and ran from the square towards the streets. Everyone was deafened by the firing.

Dr Gaspar and two others stopped on the second floor of the tower. They looked out of a narrow little window that had been knocked out of the thick wall.

Only one person could see out properly. The others looked with just one eye. And the doctor looked with one eye. But the spectacle was terrifying enough even for that one eye.

The huge iron gates were flung open to their full width. Some three hundred people flew in through the gates at once. They were artisans in grey cloth jackets with green cuffs. They were falling, bathed in blood. Guardsmen were galloping over their heads. The guardsmen were hacking with sabres and shooting from rifles. Yellow feathers were fluttering, black oilskin hats were sparkling, horses were opening wide their red jaws, turning their eyes inside out and spraying lather around.

'Look! Look! Prospero!' cried the doctor.

Prospero the armourer was being dragged along in a noose. He was walking, tumbling over, getting up again. He had tangled red hair, a blood-stained face, and his neck was encompassed by a thick noose.

'Prospero! He's been taken prisoner!' cried the doctor.

At that moment a bomb flew into the laundry. The tower leant over, rocked, lingered for a second in a slanting position, and collapsed. The doctor flew into a somersault, losing his second heel, walking stick, little case and glasses.

Ten Scaffolds

The doctor fell fortunately: he didn't crack his head open, and his legs remained intact. However, that means nothing. Even falling fortunately isn't entirely pleasant when it's along with a wounded tower, especially for a man who isn't so much young as old, as Dr Gaspar Arneri was. In any event, the doctor lost consciousness from the fright alone.

When he came to, it was already the evening. The doctor looked around.

'What a nuisance! My glasses are broken, of course. When I look at things without glasses, I see them the way a non-short-sighted person probably does if he puts glasses on. It's very unpleasant.'

Then he had a grumble about his broken heels:

'I'm not tall as it is, and now I'll be two inches shorter. Or maybe four inches, as both heels have come off? No, of course not, only two inches…'

He was lying on a pile of rubble. Almost the entire tower had fallen to pieces. A long and narrow portion of the wall was poking out like a bone. Very far away, there was music playing. A gay waltz was flying off with the wind – dying away and not returning. The doctor raised his head. From various sides up above there drooped black, broken beams. Stars were shining in the greenish evening sky.

'Where is it they're playing?' said the doctor in surprise.

It was getting cold without his cape. Not a single voice was to be heard in the square. Grunting, the doctor rose amidst the stones that had fallen down on top of one another. On his way he stumbled on somebody's large boot. The metal worker was lying stretched out across some beams and was looking into the sky. The doctor gave him a shake. The metal worker didn't want to get up. He was dead.

The doctor raised a hand to take off his hat.

'I've lost my hat too. Where ever am I to go?'

He left the square. People were lying on the road; the doctor bent low over each one and saw the stars reflected in their wide-open eyes. He touched their foreheads with the palm of his hand. They were very cold and wet with blood, which in the night-time seemed to be black.

'There! There!' whispered the doctor. 'So the people are defeated... What on earth will happen now?'

After half an hour he had reached parts where there were people about. He was very tired. He was hungry and thirsty. Here the town had a normal air.

After a lot of walking the doctor stood resting at a crossroads, and thought: 'How strange! Different coloured lights are burning, carriages are hurrying along, glass doors are jangling. Semicircular windows are radiant with golden radiance. There are couples flashing past columns. There's a merry ball going on. Coloured Chinese lanterns are spinning around above black water. People are living as they did yesterday. Don't they know about what happened this morning? Didn't they hear the firing and the groans? Don't they know that Prospero the armourer, the people's leader, has been taken prisoner? Maybe nothing actually happened? Maybe I had a bad dream?'

On the corner, where a three-armed streetlamp was burning, some carriages were standing beside the pavement. Flower-sellers were selling roses. The coachmen were exchanging remarks with the flower-sellers.

'They dragged him all through the town wearing a noose. The poor fellow!'

'Now he's been put in an iron cage. The cage is in the Palace of the Three Fat Men,' said a fat coachman in a pale-blue top hat with a bow.

Here a lady with a little girl came up to the flower-sellers to buy some roses.

'Who's been put in a cage?' she enquired.

'Prospero the armourer. The guardsmen took him prisoner.'

'Well, thank Heaven!' said the lady.

The little girl started whimpering.

'Why ever are you crying, you silly girl?' asked the lady in surprise. 'Are you sorry for Prospero the armourer? There's no need to be sorry for him. He wanted to do us harm. Look, what beautiful roses...'

Large roses like swans were floating slowly in bowls full of bitter water and leaves.

'Here are three roses for you. And there's no reason to cry. They're rebels. If they're not put in iron cages, they'll take away our houses, our dresses and our roses, and us ourselves they'll slaughter.'

At that moment a little boy ran past. First he gave a tug on the lady's star-spangled cape, and then on the little girl's plait.

'It's all right, Countess!' cried the little boy. 'Prospero the armourer's in a cage, but Tibullus the acrobat's at large.'

'Impudent wretch!'

The lady stamped her foot and dropped her bag. The flower-sellers broke into peals of laughter. The fat coachman exploited the turmoil and suggested the lady get into his carriage and go.

The lady and the little girl drove off.

'Hold on, fidget!' a flower-seller cried to the boy. 'Just come here! Tell us what you know...'

Two coachmen got down from their boxes, becoming entangled in their greatcoats with five capes attached to them, and went over to the flower-sellers.

'Now that's what I call a knout! A whacking great knout!' thought the little boy, gazing at the long whip which one of the coachmen was brandishing. The little boy really wanted to have such a knout, but for many reasons that was impossible.

'So what is it you're saying,' asked the coachman in a bass voice. 'Tibullus the acrobat's at large?'

'So they say. I was at the port...'

'Wasn't he killed by the guards?' asked the other coachman, also in a bass voice.

'No, dad… Give me a rose, beautiful!'

'Hold on, silly. You go on with the story instead…'

'Yes. Well, so then… At first everyone thought he'd been killed. Then they looked for him among the dead and didn't find him.'

'Perhaps they threw him into the canal?' asked one of the coachmen.

A beggar butted into the conversation.

'Threw who into the canal?' he asked. 'Tibullus the acrobat isn't a kitten, you can't drown him. Tibullus the acrobat's alive. He managed to escape!'

'You're lying, you camel!' said one of the coachmen.

'Tibullus the acrobat's alive!' the flower-sellers cried in delight.

The little boy pinched a rose and set off at a run. Drops of water from the wet flower were sprinkled over the doctor. The doctor wiped the drops, as bitter as tears, from his face, and went up closer to listen to what the beggar would say.

Here the conversation was disturbed by something. There appeared in the street an extraordinary procession. In front rode two horsemen with torches. The torches were fluttering like fiery beards. Next, moving along slowly, was a black carriage bearing a coat of arms.

And behind it walked carpenters. There were a hundred of them.

They walked with their sleeves rolled up, ready for work – wearing aprons, and with saws, planes and boxes under their arms. On both sides of the procession rode guardsmen. They were restraining their horses, which wanted to gallop.

'What's this? What's this?' passers-by became agitated.

In the black carriage with the coat of arms sat an official of the Council of the Three Fat Men. The flower-sellers had a fright. Lifting the palms of their hands to their cheeks, they looked at his head. It was visible through the glass door. The street was brightly lit. The black head in a wig was rocking about as though dead. It was as if there were a bird sitting in the carriage.

'Stand aside!' shouted the guardsmen.

'Where are the carpenters going?' a small flower-seller asked the senior guardsman.

And the guardsman shouted so savagely right in her face that her hair was blown about as though in a draught:

'The carpenters are going to build scaffolds! Understood? The carpenters are to build ten scaffolds!'

'Ah!'

The flower-seller dropped her bowl. The roses poured out like compote.

'They're going to build scaffolds!' Dr Gaspar repeated in horror.

'Scaffolds!' shouted the guardsman, turning and baring his teeth beneath moustaches that looked like boots. 'Scaffolds for all the rebels! They'll all have their heads chopped off! All who dare to rise up against the rule of the Three Fat Men.'

The doctor's head began to spin. He thought he was going to faint.

'I've been through too much in the course of the day,' he said to himself, 'and apart from that, I'm very hungry and very tired. I must hurry home.'

It was, indeed, time the doctor had a rest. He was so agitated by all that had happened and all he had seen and heard that he didn't even attach significance to his own flight along with the tower, or to the absence of his hat, cape, walking stick and heels. Worst of all, of course, was being without his glasses.

He hired a carriage and set off for home.

Star Circus

The doctor returned home. He rode along the widest of asphalted streets, which were lit more brightly than ballrooms, and the chain of streetlights ran high in the sky above him. The lights looked like globes filled with dazzling boiling milk. Around the lights, swarms of midges were scattered, sang and perished. He rode along an embankment, past stone walls. Here, bronze lions held shields in their paws and poked out their long tongues. Below flowed water, slow and thick, black and gleaming like pitch. The town was toppling over into the water, sinking, trying to float away, but it couldn't, it only dissolved in patches of delicate gold. He rode over bridges, curved in the form of arches. From below or from the other bank they seemed like cats, arching their iron backs before leaping. Here, by the entrance to the town, guards were posted on every bridge. The soldiers were sitting on drums, smoking pipes, playing cards, and gazing at the stars and yawning.

The doctor rode, watched and listened.

From the street, from houses, from the open windows of taverns, from behind the walls of pleasure gardens came some of the words of a little song,

> *Prospero's been fitted with*
> *A collar to curb his rage –*
> *Now the zealous armourer's*
> *Been sat in an iron cage.*

The verse was caught up by a tipsy dandy. The dandy's aunt, who had had a lot of money, even more freckles, and not a single other relation, had died. The dandy had inherited all his aunt's money. And so, of course, he wasn't pleased that the people were rising up against the rule of the rich.

There was a big show on at the menagerie. On a wooden stage, three fat, hairy apes represented the Three Fat Men. A fox terrier was playing the mandolin. A clown in a crimson costume with a golden sun on his back and a golden moon on his stomach was declaiming verse in time with the music,

Like three great sacks of wheat,
The Three Fat Men abed!
For all they do is eat
And watch their bellies spread!
Hey, you Fat Men, beware:
Your final days are here!

'Your final days are here!' cried bearded parrots on all sides.

An incredible noise arose. Creatures in various cages began barking, growling, trilling and whistling.

The apes started rushing around the stage. It was impossible to tell where their arms were and where their legs. They jumped down into the audience and went to make a run for it. There was uproar among the audience as well. Particularly noisy were those who were on the fat side. With flushed cheeks, and shaking in fury, the fat people were flinging their hats and opera glasses at the clown. A fat lady swung her umbrella about threateningly and, catching her fat neighbour with it, she tore the latter's hat off.

'Oh, oh, oh!' the neighbour started moaning, throwing her hands in the air, because along with the hat, her wig had flown off too.

As it was getting away, one of the apes slapped its palm down on the woman's bald head. Her neighbour fainted.

'Ha-ha-ha!'

'Ha-ha-ha!' roared the remainder of the audience, thinner to look at and less well-dressed. 'Bravo! Bravo! Let 'em have it!

Down with the Three Fat Men! Long live Prospero! Long live Tibullus! Long live the people!'

At that moment someone's very loud cry rang out:

'Fire! The town's on fire…'

Crushing one another and overturning benches, people ran towards the exits. Keepers tried to catch the scattering apes.

The man who was driving the doctor turned around and, pointing ahead with his knout, said:

'The guardsmen are setting the workers' districts on fire. They're trying to find Tibullus the acrobat…'

Above the town, above the black heap of houses, there trembled a pink glow.

When the doctor's carriage found itself at the town's main circus, which was called Star Circus, it proved impossible to get through. Crowding at the entrance was a mass of carriages, coaches, horsemen and pedestrians.

'What's going on?' asked the doctor.

No-one made any reply, because everyone was preoccupied with what was happening in the circus. The driver rose to his full height on the box and started gazing in that direction too.

The circus was called Star Circus for the following reason: it was surrounded by huge houses of identical height and shape, and was covered with a glass dome, which made it like a colossal circus. In the middle of the dome, at a terrifying height, burnt the largest streetlamp in the world. It was a globe of amazing size. Gripped by a horizontal iron ring and suspended on mighty hawsers, it looked like the planet Saturn. Its light was so beautiful, and so unlike any kind of earthly light, that people gave the lamp a wonderful name – the Star. And the circus as a whole began to be called that too.

Not in the circus, nor in the houses, nor in the nearby streets was any further light required. The Star lit up all the crannies, all the corners and lumber rooms in all the houses that surrounded the circus in a stone ring. The people here managed without lamps and candles.

The driver peered over the tops of the carriages, the coaches and the coachmen's tall hats, which looked like the necks of chemists' phials.

'What can you see? What's going on there?' worried the doctor, peering out from behind the coachman's back. The little doctor couldn't see anything, particularly as he was short-sighted.

The driver reported everything he saw.

And this is what he saw.

There was great agitation in the circus. People were running across the huge, round space. It was as if the ring of Star Circus were turning like a carousel. People were reeling about from one spot to another to get a better view of what was happening above.

The monstrous streetlamp, blazing on high, was dazzling for the eyes, like the sun. People were craning their necks and shading their eyes with the palms of their hands.

'There he is! There he is!' cries rang out.

'There, look! There!'

'Where? Where?'

'Higher!'

'Tibullus! Tibullus!'

Hundreds of index fingers stretched out to the left. There stood an ordinary house. But all the windows on the six floors were open. Heads were sticking out from every window. They were different to look at: some were in nightcaps with tassels; others were in pink bonnets with ringlets the colour of paraffin; others still were in kerchiefs; at the top, where young, poor people lived – poets, artists, actresses – there peered out cheerful, beardless faces in clouds of tobacco smoke, and the little heads of women, encircled by such a radiance of golden hair that it seemed as though they had wings on their shoulders. With its wide-open, little lattice windows, from which multi-coloured heads were poking out in a birdlike way, the house looked like a large cage filled with goldfinches. The owners of the heads were trying to see something very significant that was happening on the roof. It was just as impossible as seeing your own ears without a mirror. Serving as the mirror for these people who wanted to see their own roof from their own house was the crowd that was raging in the circus. It could see everything, and it shouted and waved its arms about: some expressed delight, others – indignation.

There, across the roof, a small figure was moving. It was slowly, carefully and confidently descending the slope of the triangular top of the house. The iron was making a clatter beneath its feet.

It was swinging a cape and trying to keep its balance, the way that a tightrope walker at the circus finds his balance with the help of a yellow Chinese umbrella.

It was Tibullus the acrobat.

The people cried:

'Bravo, Tibullus! Bravo, Tibullus!'

'Keep going! Remember how you walked the tightrope at the fair.'

'He won't fall! He's the best acrobat in the country…'

'It's not his first time. We've seen how skilful he is at tightrope walking…'

'Bravo, Tibullus!'

'Flee! Escape! Free Prospero!'

Others were indignant. They shook their fists:

'You won't get away, you pitiful clown!'

'Knave!'

'Rebel! You'll be shot like a rabbit…'

'Beware! We'll drag you down from the roof onto the scaffold. Ten scaffolds will be ready tomorrow!'

Tibullus continued his terrifying path.

'Where has he sprung from?' people asked. 'How did he appear in the circus? How did he get onto the roof?'

'He broke free from the guardsmen,' others replied. 'He escaped, disappeared, and then he was seen in various parts of town – he was moving over the roofs. He's as agile as a cat. His art's come in useful for him. Not for nothing has his fame spread throughout the land.'

Guardsmen appeared in the circus. Idle onlookers ran towards the side streets. Tibullus stepped over the parapet and stood on the ledge. He reached out his arm with the cape wound around it. The yellow cape fluttered like a banner.

The people were used to seeing him with this same cape, in this same leotard, fashioned out of yellow and black triangles, during performances at fairs and at Sunday fêtes.

Now, high up beneath the glass dome, small, slim and striped, he looked like a wasp crawling across the white wall of a house. When the cape fanned out it was as if the wasp were opening shiny green wings.

'You'll fall off in a minute, you vulgar knave! In a minute you'll be shot!' shouted the tipsy dandy who had had the inheritance from the freckled aunt.

The guardsmen chose a convenient position. The officer ran around, extremely preoccupied. He held a pistol in his hand. His spurs were as long as sledge runners.

Complete silence fell. The doctor clutched at his heart, which was leaping like an egg in boiling water.

Tibullus paused for a second on the ledge. He needed to get across to the opposite side of the circus. Then he could escape from Star Circus in the direction of the workers' districts.

The officer took up his position in a flowerbed in the middle of the circus, which was gay with yellow and blue flowers. There was a pool there, and a fountain which spurted out from a round stone bowl.

'Hold on!' said the officer to the soldiers. 'I'll shoot him myself. I'm the best shot in the regiment. Learn from me how you ought to shoot.'

From nine houses, from all directions, there stretched towards the middle of the dome, towards the Star, nine steel hawsers (wires as thick as a nautical cable).

It was as if from the streetlamp, from the magnificent blazing Star, nine extremely long, black rays had flown out above the circus.

It's not known what Tibullus was thinking of at that moment. But this was what he had probably decided: 'I'll cross over the circus on this wire, the way I walked on the tightrope at the fair. I won't fall. One wire stretches to the streetlamp, another from the streetlamp to the house opposite. By going across both wires I'll reach the roof opposite and escape.'

The officer raised his pistol and began to take aim. Tibullus went along the ledge as far as the spot where the wire began, parted with the wall and moved off along the wire towards the streetlamp.

The crowd gasped.

At times he went very slowly, and at times he suddenly all but broke into a run, stepping quickly and carefully, swaying a little with his arms outstretched. At every moment it seemed he would fall. Now his shadow appeared on the wall. The closer he came to the streetlamp, the lower his shadow dipped down the wall, and as it did so it became bigger and paler.

Below was an abyss.

And when he was halfway to the streetlamp, in the total silence the voice of the officer rang out:

'Now I'm going to shoot. He'll fly straight into the pool. One, two, three!'

A shot crashed out.

Tibullus continued walking, while the officer for some reason collapsed straight into the pool.

He was dead.

One of the guardsmen was holding a pistol from which light blue smoke was coming. He had shot the officer.

'Dog!' said the guardsman. 'You wanted to kill the people's friend. I prevented it. Long live the people!'

'Long live the people!' other guardsmen supported him.

'Long live the Three Fat Men!' cried their opponents.

These scattered in all directions and opened fire on the man walking along the wire.

He was now just two steps from the streetlamp. Waving the cape, Tibullus shielded his eyes from the glare. Bullets flew past. The crowd roared in delight.

Bang! Bang!

'Missed!'

'Hurrah! Missed!'

Tibullus clambered up onto the ring that went around the streetlamp.

'Never mind!' cried the guardsmen. 'He'll be crossing to the other side... He'll be going along another wire. And that's where we'll pick him off!'

Here something no one was expecting happened. The little striped figure, which in the glare of the streetlamp had become black, squatted down on the iron ring and turned some sort of lever, something gave a click, a tinkle – and the streetlamp instantly went out.

No one had time to say a word. It became terribly dark and terribly quiet, like inside a trunk.

And the next moment, ever so high up, something banged and rang once again. In the dark dome a pale square had opened up. Everyone saw a small piece of the sky with two little stars. Then into this square, against the background of the sky, there climbed a small, black figure, and someone could be heard running quickly over the glass dome.

Tibullus the acrobat had escaped from Star Circus through a hatch.

The horses were frightened by the shots and the sudden darkness.

The doctor's carriage almost overturned. The coachman turned about sharply and drove the doctor on by a roundabout route.

Thus, after going through an extraordinary day and an extraordinary night, Dr Gaspar Arneri finally returned home. His housekeeper, Auntie Ganymede, met him on the porch. She was very agitated. Indeed: the doctor had been absent so long! Auntie Ganymede threw up her hands, gasped, shook her head:

'Where on earth are your glasses? They're broken? Oh, Doctor, Doctor! Where on earth is your cape? You've lost it? Oh dear, oh dear!...'

'Auntie Ganymede, apart from that I've broken off both my heels...'

'Oh dear, what a misfortune!'

'There was a graver misfortune today, Auntie Ganymede: Prospero the armourer has been taken prisoner. He's been put in an iron cage.'

Auntie Ganymede knew nothing about what had been happening during the day. She had heard the cannon fire, and she had seen the glow above the houses. A neighbour had told her about a hundred carpenters building scaffolds for rebels in Court Square.

'I got ever so scared. I closed the shutters and decided not to go out anywhere. Lunch went cold, dinner went cold, and still you weren't home...' she added.

The night had ended. The doctor started putting himself to bed.

Amongst the hundred branches of learning that he had studied was history. The doctor had a large book in a leather binding. In that book he recorded his deliberations on important events.

'One must be meticulous,' said the doctor, raising a finger.

And, in spite of his tiredness, the doctor took his leather book, sat down at the table and began recording:

'Artisans, miners, sailors – all the poor working people of the town rose up against the rule of the Three Fat Men. The guardsmen were victorious. Prospero the armourer was taken prisoner, and Tibullus the acrobat escaped. Just now in Star Circus a guardsman shot his officer dead. That means all the soldiers will soon refuse to fight against the people or to defend the Three Fat Men. One must, however, fear for the fate of Tibullus...'

Here the doctor heard a noise behind him. He looked round. There was the fireplace. And out from the fireplace climbed a tall man in a green cape. It was Tibullus the acrobat.

Part Two

Tutti the Heir's Doll

The Amazing Adventures
of the Balloon Seller

Next day, the work was in full swing in Court Square: the carpenters were building the ten scaffolds. An escort of guardsmen was overseeing the work. The carpenters were doing their job without especial enthusiasm.

'We don't want to build scaffolds for artisans and miners!' they said indignantly.

'They're our brothers.'

'They faced death to liberate all who labour.'

'Silence!' yelled the commander of the escort in such a terrible voice that his cry made the planks prepared for the building work topple over. 'Silence, or I'll order you to be given the lash!'

Since early morning, crowds of people had been heading towards Court Square from various directions.

There was a strong wind, and dust was flying, shop signs were swinging and creaking, hats were being torn from heads and were rolling under the wheels of bouncing carriages.

In one spot something utterly unbelievable happened because of the wind: a children's balloon seller was carried away into the air by his balloons.

'Hurrah! Hurrah!' children cried, observing the fantastical flight.

They clapped their hands: firstly, the spectacle was interesting in itself, and secondly, there was a certain pleasantness for the children in the unpleasantness of the flying balloon seller's situation. The children had always been envious of the balloon seller. Envy is a bad feeling. But what can be done! The balloons, red, blue, yellow, seemed magnificent. Everyone wanted to have such a balloon. The man had a whole bunch of them. But miracles don't happen! Not once in his life had the man given one single boy, not even the most obedient, or one single girl, not even the most attentive, one single balloon: not a red one, not a blue one, not a yellow one.

Now fate had punished him for his callousness. He flew over the town, hanging from the rope to which the balloons were tied. High in the sparkling blue sky they looked like a magical flying bunch of multi-coloured grapes.

'Help!' cried the man, with no hope of anything and with his legs kicking.

On his feet he had straw shoes which were too big for him. While he had been walking about on the ground, everything had been working out all right. He had been dragging his feet along the pavement like a lazybones so that the shoes didn't fall off. But now, finding himself in the air, he was no longer able to resort to this trick.

'Damn it!'

Soaring and squeaking, the bunch of balloons was tossed about on the wind.

And one shoe did fly off after all.

'Look! A peanut! A peanut!' cried the children, running along below.

The falling shoe did, indeed, look like a peanut.

Passing down the street at that moment was a dancing-master. He seemed very elegant. He was tall, with a small round head and slender legs, and looked like either a violin or a grass-hopper. His delicate hearing, accustomed to the sad voice of the flute and the gentle words of dancers, could not bear the loud, merry cries of the band of children.

'Stop shouting!' he said angrily. 'How dare you shout so loud! Delight should be expressed in beautiful, melodic phrases... Well, for example...'

He struck a pose, but wasn't in time to give an example. Like any dancing-master, he was in the habit of looking, for the most part, down, at where he was going! Alas! He didn't see what was happening up above.

The balloon seller's shoe fell onto his head. His head was small, and the big straw shoe fitted onto it like a hat.

And now even the elegant dancing-master howled like a driver of lazy oxen.

The shoe covered up half of his face.

The children clutched at their stomachs.

'Ha-ha-ha! Ha-ha-ha!'

Dancing-master Onetwothreesir
Usually looked down,
And so he squealed just like a rat
When walking through the town –
A straw shoe fell upon his head
And made him look a clown!

Thus sang some boys who were sitting on a fence, ready to drop down onto the other side and bolt at any moment.

'Oh!' groaned the dancing-master. 'Oh, how I'm suffering! And it might at least have been a nice dancing shoe, but instead it's such a disgusting, crude one!'

It ended with the dancing-master being arrested.

'My dear man,' he was told, 'your appearance is exciting horror. You're disturbing the public peace. You shouldn't be doing that in any case, but still less at a time of such disquiet.'

The dancing-master wrung his hands.

'What a lie!' he sobbed. 'What a calumny! I, a man who lives amidst waltzes and smiles, I, whose very figure is like a treble clef – is it possible that I might disturb the public peace? Oh!... Oh!...'

What happened to the dancing-master next is unknown. And in the end it's of no interest either. It's much more important to find out what had become of the flying balloon seller.

He was flying like a good dandelion.

'This is scandalous!' wailed the balloon seller. 'I don't want to fly. I simply don't know how to fly…'

It was all useless. The wind was strengthening. The bunch of balloons rose ever higher and higher. The wind drove it beyond the town in the direction of the Palace of the Three Fat Men.

Sometimes the balloon seller managed to look down. Then he saw roofs, tiles like dirty fingernails, whole districts, blue, narrow water, chubby little people and the green mush of gardens. The town was rotating below him as if fixed on a pin.

Matters were taking a nasty turn.

'A little more, and I'll fall into the Park of the Three Fat Men!' the balloon seller thought in horror.

And the next minute he was floating slowly, sedately, and beautifully over the park, descending ever lower and lower. The wind was dropping.

'I'll quite likely be landing on the ground at any moment. I'll be seized, first I'll be given a sound beating, and then I'll be put in prison, or, to save trouble, I'll have my head chopped off at once.'

Nobody saw him. Only from one tree did some frightened birds spurt out in all directions. From the flying, multi-coloured bunch of balloons there fell a light, airy shadow like the shadow of a cloud. Translucent with cheerful rainbow colours, it slid over a gravel-strewn path, a flowerbed, a statue of a boy sitting on a goose, and a guardsman who had fallen asleep on duty. And it made wonderful changes take place on the guardsman's face. His nose at once became as blue as a dead man's, then as green as a conjuror's, and, finally, as red as a drunkard's. This is the way that, changing hue, the glass shifts around in a kaleidoscope.

The fateful moment was approaching: the balloon seller was heading towards the open windows of the palace. He had no doubt that he was about to fly in through one of them like a bit of fluff.

And that is just what did happen.

The balloon seller flew in through a window. And the window proved to be a window of the palace kitchen. It was the confectionary.

A gala luncheon was planned in the Palace of the Three Fat Men that day on the occasion of the successful suppression of the previous day's revolt. After the luncheon, the Three Fat Men, the entire State Council, their suite and guests of honour were intending to drive to Court Square.

To get into the palace confectionary, my friends, is a very tempting thing. The Fat Men knew their stuff in eats. What's more, the occasion was exceptional too. A gala luncheon! You can imagine what interesting work the palace cooks and confectioners were doing that day.

Flying into the confectionary, the balloon seller felt at one and the same time both horror and delight. A wasp is probably both horrified and delighted in the same way when flying towards a cake which has been stood out on the windowsill by a careless housewife.

He was only flying for a moment, and didn't have time to make anything out properly. At first it seemed to him that he was in some amazing aviary, where precious multi-coloured birds from southern lands were bustling about, singing and whistling, hissing and chattering. But the next instant he thought that it wasn't an aviary, but a fruit shop, full of tropical fruits, squashed, oozing, engulfed in their own juice. A sweet, dizzying fragrance struck him in the nose; heat and stuffiness squeezed at his throat.

And then everything got mixed up: both the amazing aviary and the fruit shop.

The balloon seller came down with all his weight into something soft and warm. He didn't let go of the balloons. He held on tight to the rope. The balloons stopped motionless above his head.

He screwed his eyes up and decided not to open them – not for anything in the world.

'Now I understand everything,' he thought, 'it's not an aviary and not a fruit shop. It's a confectionary. And I'm sitting in a cake!'

And so it was.

He was sitting in a realm of chocolate, oranges, pomegranates, butter cream, candied fruit, castor sugar and jam, and he was sitting on a throne, like the sovereign of a heavily scented, multi-coloured realm. And the throne was a cake.

He didn't open his eyes. He was expecting an unbelievable uproar, a storm – and was ready for anything. But what happened was something that he hadn't expected at all.

'The cake's done for,' said the junior confectioner, sternly and sadly.

Then silence fell. There were just the bubbles bursting on boiling chocolate.

'What's going to happen?' whispered the balloon seller, gasping for breath in terror, and squeezing up his eyelids till they hurt.

His heart was leaping like a penny in a piggy bank.

'Nonsense!' said the senior confectioner, just as severely. 'They've eaten the main course in the hall. In twenty minutes' time the cake has to be served. Multi-coloured balloons and the stupid face of this flying scoundrel will be a splendid decoration for the gala cake.'

And after saying this, the confectioner yelled:

'Give me the butter cream!...'

And the butter cream was, indeed, given.

And what a thing happened!

Three confectioners and twenty kitchen-lads threw themselves upon the balloon seller with a zeal that was worthy of the praise of the very fattest of the Three Fat Men.

In a minute he had been plastered on all sides. He sat with his eyes closed, so *he* could see nothing, but the spectacle was monstrous. He was completely plastered over. Sticking out were just his head and his round face, which looked like a teapot decorated with daisies. The remainder was covered with white butter cream which had a delightful pink tint. The balloon seller might have seemed like anything you wanted, but he had lost his resemblance to himself, just as he had lost his straw shoe.

A poet might now have taken him for a swan in snow-white plumage, a gardener for a marble statue, a laundress for a mountain of soapy foam and a naughty child for a snowman.

Above hung the balloons. The decoration was something out of the ordinary, but, nonetheless, all together it made up quite an interesting picture.

'Right,' said the head confectioner in the tone of an artist admiring his own picture.

And then his voice became savage, just like the first time, as he yelled:

'Candied fruit!!'

Candied fruit appeared of all sorts, of all shapes, of all sizes: rather bitter, vanilla-flavoured, slightly sour, triangular, little stars, round, crescent-shaped, little roses.

The kitchen-lads worked flat out. The head confectioner wasn't able to clap his hands three times before the whole pile of butter cream, the whole cake was studded all over with candied fruit.

'It's all ready,' said the head confectioner. 'Now I suppose we ought to put it in the oven to brown a little.'

'In the oven?' thought the balloon seller in horror. 'What? What oven? Me in the oven?'

At this point one of the servants ran into the kitchen.

'The cake! The cake!' he cried. 'The cake, at once! They're waiting for dessert in the hall!'

'It's all ready!' replied the head confectioner.

'Thank God!' thought the balloon seller. Now he opened his eyes just a very little.

Six servants in pale-blue livery picked up the huge dish on which he was sitting. They carried him off. As he was moving away, he heard the kitchen-lads having a good laugh at him.

He was carried up a wide staircase into the hall. For a second he screwed his eyes up again. The hall was noisy and merry. There was the sound of many voices, and the rumble of laughter and applause could be heard. All the signs were that the gala luncheon had been a great success.

The balloon seller or, rather, the cake, was brought in and set down on a table.

Then the balloon seller opened his eyes.

And at once he saw the Three Fat Men.

They were so fat that the balloon seller's mouth fell open.

'I must shut it at once,' he realised immediately. 'In my position, better not show any sign of life.'

But – alas! – his mouth wouldn't shut. And so it continued for two minutes. Then his surprise lessened. With an effort he closed his mouth. But then immediately his eyes popped out. With great difficulty, shutting by turns now his mouth, now his eyes, he did finally overcome his surprise.

The Fat Men were sitting in the places of honour, towering over the remainder of the company.

They ate more than anyone. One even started to eat his napkin.

'You're eating your napkin…'

'Really? I got carried away…'

He left the napkin alone, and at once set about chewing the ear of the Third Fat Man. Mind you, it did look like a curd dumpling.

Everyone burst into roars of laughter.

'Let's cut out the jokes,' said the Second Fat Man, raising his fork. 'Things are taking a serious turn. They've brought the cake.'

'Hurrah!'

There was a general increase in animation.

'What's going to happen?' the balloon seller agonised. 'What's going to happen? They'll eat me!'

At that moment the clock struck two.

'The executions in Court Square will begin in an hour,' said the First Fat Man.

'The first to be executed will, of course, be Prospero the armourer?' asked one of the guests of honour.

'He won't be executed today,' replied the State Chancellor.

'What? What? Why not?'

'We're keeping him alive for the time being. We want to find out from him the rebels' plans and the names of the chief conspirators.'

'And where is he now?'

The entire company was most interested, and they had even forgotten about the cake.

'He's sitting in an iron cage, as before. The cage is here, in the palace, in Tutti the Heir's menagerie.'

'Summon him...'

'Bring him here!' cried the guests.

'Yes, that's right,' said the First Fat Man. 'Let our guests take a look at this animal close to. I'd invite everyone to go to the menagerie. But there's roaring and squealing there, and it stinks. It's much worse than the clinking of glasses and the smells of the fruit...'

'Of course! Of course! It's not worth going to the menagerie...'

'Have Prospero brought here. We'll eat the cake and take a good look at the monster.'

'Again, the cake!' the balloon seller took fright. 'They're obsessed with this cake... The gluttons!'

'Bring Prospero here,' said the First Fat Man.

As the State Chancellor left the room, the servants, who stood forming a corridor, moved apart and bowed – the height of the corridor was halved.

The gluttons fell quiet.

'He's really scary,' said the Second Fat Man. 'He's stronger than anyone else. He's stronger than a lion. Hatred burns right through his eyes. No one has the strength to look into them.'

'He's got an awful head,' said the Secretary to the State Council. 'It's enormous. It looks like the capital of a column. He's got red hair. You might think his head's enveloped in flame.'

Now that a conversation had begun about Prospero the armourer, a change had come over the gluttons. They had stopped eating, joking and making a noise, they had pulled in their stomachs, and some had even turned pale. Many were already unhappy about having wanted to see him.

The Three Fat Men had grown serious, and it was as if they had become slightly slimmer.

Suddenly everyone fell silent. Absolute quiet set in. Each of the Fat Men made a movement as though wanting to hide behind one of the others.

Prospero the armourer was led into the hall.

In front walked the State Chancellor. To the sides, guardsmen. They came in still wearing their black oilskin hats and holding drawn sabres. A chain was clanking. The armourer's hands were shackled. He was led up to the table. He stopped a few paces away from the Fat Men.

Prospero the armourer stood with his head lowered. The prisoner was pale. There was dried blood on his forehead and temples beneath his tangled red hair.

He raised his head and looked at the Fat Men. All the people sitting close by recoiled.

'What have you brought him here for?' came the cry of one of the guests. He was the country's richest miller. 'I'm scared of him!'

And the miller fainted, with his nose going straight into his blancmange. Some of the guests rushed to the exits. No one was concerned with the cake any longer.

'What do you want of me?' asked the armourer.

The First Fat Man plucked up his courage.

'We wanted to take a look at you,' he said. 'And aren't you interested in seeing the people in whose hands you find yourself?'

'I find seeing you offensive.'

'We'll soon be chopping your head off. That way we'll help you to avoid seeing us.'

'I'm not afraid. Mine is just one head. The people have hundreds of thousands of heads. You won't be able to chop *them* off.'

'There's an execution today in Court Square. There the executioners will make short work of your comrades.'

The gluttons had a little grin. The miller came to, and even licked the blancmange roses off his cheeks.

'Your brain's all smothered in fat,' said Prospero. 'You can't see anything beyond your own belly…'

'Well, fancy that!' said the Second Fat Man, offended. 'And so what ought we to see?'

'Ask your ministers. They know about what's happening in the country.'

The State Chancellor gave an indeterminate quack. The ministers began drumming their fingers on their plates.

'Ask them,' Prospero continued, 'they'll tell you…'

He paused. Everyone pricked up their ears.

'They'll tell you about how the peasants from whom you take the grain, won by hard labour, are rising up against the landowners. They're burning down their palaces, they're driving them off their land. The miners don't want to extract coal just for you to take possession of it. The workers are breaking machines so as not to work for the sake of your enrichment. The sailors are throwing your cargoes away into the sea. The soldiers are refusing to serve you. Scholars, officials, judges, actors are crossing over to the people's side. All who used to work for you and were paid peanuts for it while you grew fat, all the unfortunate, the deprived, the hungry, the emaciated ones, the orphans, the cripples, the beggars – all are going to war with you, with the fat and the rich who have replaced their hearts with stone…'

'I think he's talking too much,' the State Chancellor intervened.

But Prospero kept on talking:

'For fifteen years I've been teaching the people to hate you and your rule. Oh, how long have we been gathering our strength! And now your final hour has come…'

'Enough!' squeaked the Third Fat Man.

'He needs to be put back in the cage,' suggested the Second one.

And the First one said:

'You'll stay in your cage until we've caught Tibullus the acrobat. We'll execute you together. The people will see your corpses. Their desire to make war against us will fade for a very long time.'

Prospero was silent. He lowered his head once more.

The Fat Man continued:

'You've forgotten who you want to make war with. We, the Three Fat Men, are strong and powerful. Everything belongs to us. I, the First Fat Man, own all the grain that our earth produces, all the coal belongs to the Second Fat Man, and the

Third has bought up all the iron. We're richer than anyone else. The richest man in the country is a hundred times poorer than us. With our gold we can buy everything we want.'

Here the gluttons flew into a frenzy. The Fat Man's words lent them courage.

'Into the cage with him! Into the cage!' they started shouting.

'Back to the menagerie!'

'Into the cage!'

'Rebel!'

'Into the cage!'

Prospero was led away.

'And now we'll eat the cake,' said the First Fat Man.

'It's the end!' the balloon seller decided.

Everyone's gaze was turned upon him. He closed his eyes. The gluttons were enjoying themselves.

'Ho-ho-ho!'

'Ha-ha-ha! What a wonderful cake! Look at the balloons!'

'They're delightful!'

'Look at that face!'

'It's marvellous!'

Everyone moved towards the cake.

'And what's inside this funny looking thing?' someone asked, and gave the balloon seller a painful flick on the forehead.

'Sweets, probably.'

'Or champagne...'

'Fascinating! Fascinating!'

'Let's cut this head off first and see what happens...'

'Ouch!'

The balloon seller couldn't contain himself, said very distinctly: 'Ouch!', and opened his eyes wide.

The inquisitive guests recoiled. And at that moment the loud cry of a child rang out in the gallery:

'The doll! My doll!'

Everyone listened closely. The Three Fat Men and the State Chancellor grew particularly agitated.

The cry turned into crying. An aggrieved child was crying loudly in the gallery.

'What is it?' asked the First Fat Man. 'That's Tutti the Heir crying!'

'That's Tutti the Heir crying!' the Second and Third Fat Men repeated as one.

All three turned pale. They were most alarmed.

The State Chancellor, several ministers and the servants rushed to the exit to the gallery.

'What is it? What is it?' a whispering began in the hall.

A boy ran into the hall. He pushed the ministers and servants aside. He ran up to the Fat Men with his hair shaking and his patent leather shoes sparkling. Through his sobs he cried out individual words which nobody could understand.

'The little boy will see me!' the balloon seller began to worry. 'The accursed butter cream, which is preventing me from breathing or moving so much as a finger, will be very much to the liking of a little boy, of course. To stop him crying, he will, of course, have a piece of cake cut for him, and along with it – my heel.'

But the boy didn't even look at the cake. Even the wonderful balloons hanging over the round head of the balloon seller failed to attract his attention.

He was crying bitterly.

'What's the matter?' asked the First Fat Man.

'Why is Tutti the Heir crying?' asked the Second one.

And the Third one blew out his cheeks.

Tutti the Heir was twelve. He was being brought up in the palace of the Three Fat Men. He was growing up like a little prince. The Fat Men wanted to have an heir. They had no children. All of the Three Fat Men's riches and the government of the country were to pass to Tutti the Heir.

Tutti the Heir's tears inspired greater fear in the Fat Men than the words of Prospero the armourer.

The boy was clenching his fists, swinging them around and stamping his feet. There was no end to his fury and injured feelings.

Nobody knew the reason.

His tutors were peering out from behind pillars, scared to enter the hall. These tutors in their black clothes and black wigs looked like the glasses of lamps, covered in soot.

In the end, when he had calmed down a little, the boy told them what was wrong.

'My doll, my wonderful doll is broken!... My doll's been ruined. The guardsmen have been stabbing my doll with their sabres...'

Again he began sobbing. He rubbed his eyes with his little fists and smeared the tears all over his cheeks.

'What?!' the Fat Men yelled.

'What?!'

'The guardsmen?'

'Stabbing it?'

'With their sabres?'

'Tutti the Heir's doll?'

And the entire hall said quietly, as though in a sigh:

'It's not possible!'

The State Chancellor took his head in his hands. That same highly-strung miller fainted again, but was brought round instantly by the terrible cry of one of the Fat Men:

'Stop the celebration! Postpone all business! Summon the Council! All the officials! All the judges! All the ministers! All the executioners! Cancel today's execution! There's treachery in the palace!'

A commotion ensued. A minute later the palace carriages hurtled off in all directions. Five minutes later, racing towards the palace from all directions were the judges, councillors and executioners. The crowd awaiting the execution of the rebels in Court Square had to disperse. Town criers, mounting the scaffold, informed the crowd that the execution was being carried over to the following day because of very important events.

The balloon seller was borne out of the hall along with the cake. The gluttons sobered up instantly.

Everyone clustered around Tutti the Heir and listened.

'I was sitting on the grass in the park, and the doll was sitting next to me. We wanted there to be a solar eclipse. It's a very interesting thing. I was reading in a book yesterday. When an eclipse takes place, stars appear in the daytime…'

The Heir couldn't speak for sobbing. And instead of him, a tutor told the whole story. He spoke with difficulty too, however, because he was trembling with fear.

'I wasn't far away from Tutti the Heir and his doll. I was sitting in the sun with my nose in the air. I have a pimple on my nose, and I thought the rays of the sun would help me get rid of the ugly pimple. And suddenly some guardsmen appeared. There were twelve of them. They were talking about something excitedly. As they drew level with us they stopped. They looked threatening. Pointing at Tutti the Heir, one of them said: "That's the wolf cub sitting there. The three lardy pigs have got a wolf cub growing up." Alas! I realised what those words had meant.'

'And who are these three lardy pigs?' asked the First Fat Man.

The other two blushed deeply. Then the First one blushed as well. All three were breathing so heavily that the glass door onto the veranda kept blowing open, then shutting.

'They clustered around Tutti the Heir,' the tutor continued. 'They said: "The three pigs are raising an iron wolf cub." – "Tutti," they asked, "what side's your heart on? His heart's been removed. He has to grow up vicious, callous and cruel, with hatred for people... When the three pigs snuff it, the vicious wolf is to take their place."'

'And why didn't you put an end to that terrible talk?' cried the State Chancellor, shaking the tutor by the shoulder. 'Didn't you work out that they were traitors who'd gone over to the side of the people?'

The tutor was horrified. He babbled:

'I could see it, but I was afraid of them. They were very excited. And I didn't have any weapon other than my pimple... They were holding on to the hilts of their sabres, ready for anything. "Look," one of them said, "there's a stuffed dummy. There's a doll. The wolf-cub plays with a doll. They don't let him see any living children. They've given him a stuffed dummy for a comrade, a doll with a spring." Then another one shouted: "I left a son and a wife in the country. My boy fired his catapult and hit a pear hanging on a tree in the landowner's park. The landowner ordered the boy to be birched for the insult to the authority of the rich, and his servants put my wife in the pillory." The guardsmen started shouting and advanced on Tutti the Heir. The one who'd told the story of the boy drew his sabre and stuck it into the doll. The others did the same...'

At this point in the story Tutti the Heir dissolved in tears.

'"There you are, wolf cub!" they said. "We'll get to your lardy pigs too later on."'

'Where are these traitors?' the Fat Men thundered.

'They dropped the doll and ran into the depths of the park. They were shouting: "Long live Prospero the armourer! Long live Tibullus the acrobat! Down with the Three Fat Men!"'

'Why ever did the bodyguards not shoot at them?' the hall asked indignantly.

And then the tutor told them a fearful thing:

'The bodyguards waved their hats to them. From behind a wall I saw the bodyguards saying goodbye to them. They were saying: "Comrades! Go to the people and say that all the troops will soon come over to their side..."'

That was what had happened in the park.

Now there was alarm. The most reliable sections of the palace guard were posted all through the palace, in the park by the entrances and exits, on the bridges and along the road to the town gates.

The State Council gathered for a meeting. The guests dispersed. The Three Fat Men were weighed on the head palace doctor's scales. It turned out that, despite the agitation, they hadn't lost a drop of lard. The head doctor was put under arrest on bread and water.

Tutti the Heir's doll was found in the park, on the grass. It hadn't survived to see a solar eclipse. It was damaged beyond hope.

Tutti the Heir was quite unable to calm himself. He hugged the broken doll and sobbed. The doll had looked like a little girl. It had been the same height as Tutti – an expensive, artfully made doll that had differed not one bit in appearance from a living girl.

Now its dress was torn to pieces, and on its breast were the black holes of the sabre blows. Just an hour before it had been able to sit, stand, smile and dance. Now it had become a simple stuffed dummy, a rag. Somewhere in its throat and in its breast, beneath the pink silk, its broken spring was wheezing, the way an old clock does before striking the time.

'She's dead,' complained Tutti the Heir. 'What a calamity! She's dead.'

Little Tutti was no wolf cub.

'The doll has to be repaired,' said the State Chancellor at the meeting of the State Council. 'Tutti the Heir's sorrow knows no bounds. The doll must be repaired at all costs.'

'A new one should be bought,' the ministers suggested.

'Tutti the Heir doesn't want another doll. He wants this doll to come back to life.'

'But who on earth can repair it?'

'I know,' said the Minister of Public Education.

'Who?'

'We have forgotten, gentlemen, that Dr Gaspar Arneri lives in town. That man can do anything. He will repair Tutti the Heir's doll.'

There was an outpouring of general delight:

'Bravo! Bravo!'

And the whole State Council, remembering Dr Gaspar, began singing in chorus:

> *How to catch a fox by the tail,*
> *How to fly from earth to a star,*
> *How to make hot steam from a stone –*
> *All is known by Dr Gaspar.*

An order was drawn up at once for Dr Gaspar.

To Dr Gaspar Arneri

Forwarding herewith the damaged doll of Tutti the Heir, the State Council of the Government of the Three Fat Men instructs you to repair this doll by tomorrow. In the event of the doll regaining its former healthy and lifelike appearance, you will be granted the reward you desire; in the event of non-fulfilment, severe punishment threatens.

President of the State Council

The State Chancellor...

And here the Chancellor signed it. The large state seal was affixed at once. It was round, with an image of a bulging sack.

The Captain of the Palace Guard, Count Bonaventura, accompanied by two guardsmen, set off for town to seek out Dr Gaspar Arneri and give him the State Council's order.

They galloped on horseback, and behind them drove a carriage. In it sat a court official. He held the doll on his lap. It nestled its wonderful head with its cropped curls sadly against his shoulder.

Tutti the Heir stopped crying. He believed that tomorrow they would bring him a revived, healthy doll.

Thus the day in the palace passed anxiously.

But how did the adventures of the flying balloon seller end?

He was taken away from the hall – that we know.

He found himself back in the confectionary.

And at that point a catastrophe occurred.

One of the servants carrying the cake stepped on a piece of orange peel.

'Hold on!' cried the servants.

'Help!' cried the balloon seller, sensing that his throne was rocking.

But the servant couldn't keep his feet. He crashed down onto the hard tiled floor. He lifted his long legs up and let out a protracted howl.

'Hurrah!' cried the kitchen-lads in delight.

'Little devils!' said the balloon seller, hopeless and forlorn, as he followed the servant in falling to the floor, along with the dish and the cake.

The dish was smashed to smithereens. The butter cream flew like snowballs in all directions. The servant leapt up and fled.

The kitchen-lads were jumping up and down, dancing and yelling.

The balloon seller sat on the floor amidst the splinters of the dish, in a puddle of raspberry syrup, and in clouds of good French butter cream, melting sadly on the ruins of the cake.

He was relieved to see that only the kitchen-lads were in the confectionary, and the three head confectioners weren't.

'I'll make a deal with the kitchen-lads, and they'll help me escape,' he decided. 'My balloons will save me.'

He was holding on tight to the string with the balloons.

The kitchen-lads clustered around him on all sides. He could see by their eyes that the balloons were treasure, that to possess even one balloon was a dream and a joy for a kitchen-lad.

He said:

'I'm very tired of adventures. I'm not a little boy or a hero. I don't like flying, I'm scared of the Three Fat Men, and I don't know how to be decorative in ceremonial cakes. I really want to rid the palace of my presence.'

The kitchen-lads had stopped laughing. The balloons swayed and spun around. This movement made the sunlight flare up inside them, at times with a blue, at times with a yellow, at times with a red flame. They were wonderful balloons.

'Can you arrange my escape?' the balloon seller asked, jerking on the rope.

'We can,' said one of the kitchen-lads quietly. And he added: 'Give us your balloons.'

The balloon seller turned pale.

'Very well,' he said in a tone of indifference, 'I agree. The balloons are very expensive. I really need these balloons, but I agree. I like you. You have such cheerful, open faces and ringing voices.' And mentally he added here: 'The devil take you!'

'The head confectioner's in the storeroom now,' said the kitchen-lad. 'He's weighing out the ingredients for the biscuits for evening tea. We need to get it done before he comes back.'

'Quite right,' agreed the balloon seller, 'there's no point in delaying.'

'Right away. I know a secret.'

With these words, the kitchen-lad went up to a large copper saucepan standing on a tiled cube, and then he lifted the lid.

'Give us the balloons,' he demanded.

'You're out of your mind,' the balloon seller grew angry. 'What do I want with your saucepan? I want to escape. What, I'm to climb into the saucepan, am I?'

'Exactly.'

'Into the saucepan?'

'Into the saucepan.'

'And then?'

'You'll see. Climb into the saucepan. It's the very best means of escape.'

The saucepan was so voluminous that not only could the skinny balloon seller climb into it, even the very fattest of the Three Fat Men could have done so.

'Hurry up and climb in, if you want to be in time.'

The balloon seller glanced into the saucepan. There was no bottom to it. He saw a black abyss, as in a well.

'All right,' he sighed. 'Into the saucepan it is. It's no worse than a flight through the air or a butter cream bath. And so goodbye, you little scoundrels. Have the price of my freedom.'

'He untied the knot and gave out the balloons to the kitchen-lads. There were enough for everyone: exactly twenty, each on a separate string.

Then, with his characteristic clumsiness, he climbed into the saucepan, feet first. A kitchen-lad slammed the lid down.

'Balloons! Balloons!' cried the kitchen-lads in delight.

They ran out of the kitchen and down the stairs to a lawn in the park, right under the windows of the confectionary.

It was much more fun playing with the balloons here in the open air.

But suddenly, in the three windows of the confectionary there appeared the three confectioners.

'What?!' each of them thundered. 'What's all this? What's this mayhem? Quick march back here!'

The kitchen-lads were so frightened by the shouting that they let go of the strings.

Happiness was at an end.

Twenty balloons flew quickly upwards, into the radiant blue sky. And the kitchen-lads stood on the grass below, surrounded by sweet peas, with their heads in white caps thrown back and their mouths agape.

A Black Man and a Head of Cabbage

You remember that the doctor's alarming night ended with the appearance from out of the fireplace of the tightrope walker and acrobat Tibullus.

What they did together at dawn in Dr Gaspar's workshop is unknown. Auntie Ganymede, exhausted by anxiety and the long wait for Dr Gaspar, slept soundly and dreamt about a chicken.

The next day – that is, the very day when the children's balloon seller flew into the Palace of the Three Fat Men, and when the guardsmen stabbed holes in Tutti the Heir's doll – something unpleasant happened to Auntie Ganymede. She let a mouse out of a mousetrap. The previous night, that mouse had eaten a pound of fruit jelly. Earlier still, during Friday night, it had overturned a glass of carnations. The glass had broken, and the carnations had for some reason picked up the smell of valerian drops.

During the alarming night, the mouse was caught.

Rising early in the morning, Auntie Ganymede picked up the mousetrap. The mouse was sitting there with an air of extreme indifference, as though it weren't the first time it had been behind bars. It was putting it on.

'Don't eat the fruit jelly another time, if it doesn't belong to you!' said Auntie Ganymede, putting the mousetrap down where it could be seen.

After getting dressed, Auntie Ganymede set off for Dr Gaspar's workshop. She was meaning to share the good news with him. The previous morning, Dr Gaspar had expressed his sympathy to her regarding the loss of the fruit jelly.

'The mouse likes the fruit jelly because there are lots of acids in it,' he had said.

This had consoled Auntie Ganymede.

'So the mouse likes my acids... We'll see if it likes my mousetrap.'

Auntie Ganymede approached the door leading into the workshop. She held the mousetrap in her hands.

It was early morning. The greenery was sparkling through the open window. The wind which carried the balloon seller away that morning only got up later on.

On the other side of the door, movement could be heard.

'The poor thing!' thought Auntie Ganymede. 'Didn't he get to bed at all?'

She knocked.

The doctor said something, but she didn't catch what.

The door opened. On the threshold stood Dr Gaspar. The workshop smelt of something like burnt cork. In the corner, twinkling as it burned out, was the red light of a crucible.

Dr Gaspar had evidently been busy for the remainder of the night with some sort of scientific work.

'Good morning!' said the doctor cheerfully.

Auntie Ganymede lifted the mousetrap up high. The mouse was sniffing the air, twitching its little nose.

'I've caught the mouse!'

'Oh!' the doctor was very pleased. 'Show me!'

Auntie Ganymede took quick little steps to the window.

'There it is!'

Auntie held out the mousetrap. And suddenly she saw a black man. Beside the window, on a crate bearing the inscription: 'With care!', sat a handsome black man.

The black man was half-naked.

The black man was wearing short red trousers.

The black man was black, purple, brown, shiny.

The black man was smoking a pipe.

Auntie Ganymede gasped so loudly that she almost tore herself in half. She spun around like a top and flung her arms up like a kitchen-garden scarecrow. In so doing, she made a clumsy sort of movement, the catch of the mousetrap gave a tinkle and came open, and the mouse fell out, disappearing who knows where.

Such was Auntie Ganymede's horror.

The black man roared with laughter, stretching out his long, bare legs with their red shoes like gigantic red peppers.

The pipe leapt up and down between his teeth like a branch in the gusts of a storm. And the doctor's glasses leapt up and down and flashed. He was laughing too.

Auntie Ganymede flew headlong out of the room.

'The mouse!' she wailed. 'The mouse! The fruit jelly! A black man!'

Dr Gaspar hurried in pursuit of her.

'Auntie Ganymede,' he reassured her, 'there's nothing for you to worry about. I forgot to warn you about my new experiment. But you might have expected something. After all, I'm a scholar, I'm a doctor of various branches of learning, I'm a master of various instruments. I conduct all sorts of experiments. In my workshop you might see not only a black man, but even an elephant. Auntie Ganymede… Auntie Ganymede… A black man is one thing, but scrambled eggs are another… We're waiting for breakfast. My black man likes a lot of scrambled eggs…'

'The mouse likes acids,' Auntie Ganymede whispered in horror, 'and the black man likes scrambled eggs…'

'There you are. The scrambled eggs now, and the mouse tonight. It'll be caught tonight, Auntie Ganymede… There's nothing left for it to do when it's at large. The fruit jelly has been eaten once and for all.'

Auntie Ganymede cried, adding tears to the scrambled eggs instead of salt. They were so bitter that they even stood in for pepper.

'A lot of pepper's a good thing. Delicious!' the black man praised the scrambled eggs as he tucked into them.

Auntie Ganymede took some valerian drops, which now for some reason smelt of carnations, probably for the tears.

Then through the window she saw Dr Gaspar going down the street. Everything was in order: a new scarf, a new walking stick, new (albeit old) shoes on smart, complete heels.

But walking next to him was the black man.

Auntie Ganymede screwed up her eyes and sat down on the floor. Or rather, not on the floor, but on the cat. The cat yowled in horror. Auntie Ganymede, at her wits' end by now, gave the cat a beating: firstly, for getting under her feet, and secondly, for not managing to catch the mouse when it should have.

And the mouse, having made its way from Dr Gaspar's workshop to Auntie Ganymede's chest of drawers, was eating almond biscuits and enjoying tender memories of the fruit jelly.

Dr Gaspar Arneri lived on Shadow Street. Turning off this street to the left, you enter a side road bearing the name of Widow Lizaveta, and from there, by cutting across a street renowned for an oak tree which had been struck by lightning, after walking for another five minutes, you could get to the Fourteenth Market.

Dr Gaspar and the black man headed in that direction. The wind was already getting up. The mangled oak tree creaked like a swing. A billposter was quite unable to manage the sheet he had prepared to stick up. The wind was tearing it out of his hands and tossing it into his face. It seemed from a distance as if the man were wiping his face with a white napkin.

Finally he succeeded in slapping the poster onto a fence.

Dr Gaspar read:

Citizens! Citizens! Citizens!

Today the Government of the Three Fat Men is organising a festival for the people. Hurry to the Fourteenth Market! Hurry! There will be spectacles, amusements, shows! Hurry!

'Right,' said Dr Gaspar, 'it's quite clear. The execution of the rebels will be today in Court Square. The Three Fat Men's executioners will cut off the heads of those who have risen against the rule of the rich and the gluttonous. The Three Fat Men mean to deceive the people. They're afraid that if the people gather in Court Square, they might break down the scaffolds, kill the executioners and free their brothers who have been condemned to death. That's why they're organising amusements for the people. They mean to distract their attention from today's execution.'

Dr Gaspar and his black companion arrived at the market square. People were jostling beside the booths. Not one dandy, not one lady in fine clothes the colours of goldfish and grapes, not one aristocratic old man in a gold-embroidered litter, not one merchant with a huge leather purse at his side did Dr Gaspar see amongst the people who had gathered.

Here were the poor residents of the outer districts of town: artisans, workmen, rye flat cake sellers, chars, dockers, elderly women, beggars, cripples. Old, grey, ragged clothing was only brightened up here and there by green cuffs, or a vivid cape, or coloured ribbons.

The wind puffed the old women's grey hair out like felt, it stung the eyes and tore at the brown rags of the beggars.

Everyone's face was gloomy, everyone was expecting something bad to happen.

'The execution's in Court Square,' people were saying. 'There the heads of our comrades will be dropping, while here the clowns who've been paid lots of gold by the Three Fat Men will be fooling around.'

'Let's go to Court Square!' cries rang out.

'We have no weapons. We have no pistols or sabres. And Court Square is surrounded by a ring of guardsmen three deep.'

'The soldiers are still doing their duty for the time being. They've been shooting at us. But it's all right! Any day now they'll be marching with us against their masters.'

'Last night in Star Circus a guardsman shot his officer. By doing so, he saved the life of Tibullus the acrobat.'

'And where is Tibullus? Did he manage to escape?'

'No one knows. All night and at dawn, guardsmen were setting the workers' districts on fire. They were trying to find him.'

Dr Gaspar and the black man approached the booths. The performance hadn't yet begun. Behind the gaudy curtains and screens, voices could be heard, bells were ringing, flutes were singing, things were squeaking, rustling and growling. Actors were preparing there for the show.

Curtains parted and a face looked out. It was a Spaniard, a crack shot with a pistol. His moustache was bristling and one eye was rolling.

'Ah,' he said, catching sight of the black man, 'are you taking part in the performance too? How much were you paid?'

The black man was silent.

'I was given ten gold pieces,' boasted the Spaniard. He had taken the black man for an actor. 'Come here,' he said in a whisper, pulling a mysterious face.

The black man went up to the curtain. The Spaniard told him a secret. It turned out that the Three Fat Men had hired a hundred actors to perform that day at the markets and to extol in every possible way in their acts the rule of the rich and gluttonous, and at the same time to decry the rebels, Prospero the armourer and Tibullus the acrobat.

'They've assembled an entire troupe: conjurors, animal tamers, clowns, horsewomen, ventriloquists, dancers... Money's been handed out to all of them.'

'And did all of the actors agree to extol the Three Fat Men?' asked Dr Gaspar.

The Spaniard hissed: 'Ssh!' he pressed a finger to his lips. 'You mustn't talk too loudly about that. Many refused. They were arrested.'

The black man spat vehemently.

At that moment music started playing. The performances had begun in some of the booths. The crowd stirred.

'Citizens!' cried the squeaky voice of a clown from a wooden stage. 'Citizens! Let me congratulate you...'

He paused, waiting for silence to fall. Flour was flaking off his face.

'Citizens, let me congratulate you on the following joyous event: today, our dear, pink Three Fat Men's executioners will cut off the heads of the dastardly rebels...'

He didn't finish what he was saying. A workman let fly at him with a half-eaten flat cake. It stuck right over his mouth.

'M-m-m-m-m-m...'

The clown mooed, but nothing could be done. The under-cooked, half-raw dough had stuck right over his mouth. He waved his arms about and frowned.

'That's it! Quite right!' shouted people in the crowd.

The clown bolted behind a screen.

'The good-for-nothing! He's sold himself to the Three Fat

Men! In return for money he's abusing the men who went to face death for the sake of our freedom!'

The music began playing louder. Several more bands had joined in: nine fifes, three bugles, three Turkish drums and a fiddle, the noise of which gave you toothache.

The owners of the booths were trying to drown out the noise of the crowd with the music.

'Our actors may get alarmed about those flat cakes,' one of them said. 'We must pretend nothing's happened.'

'Come along! Come along! The show's beginning…'

Another booth was called 'The Trojan Horse'.

Out from behind the curtain came the showman. On his head was a very tall hat made of heavy green cloth, on his chest were round brass buttons, on his cheeks was a painstakingly drawn, handsome flush.

'Quiet!' he said, as though he were speaking German. 'Quiet! Our performance is worthy of your attention.'

Attention of a sort was established.

'To mark today's celebration we have for you the strongman Lapitup.'

'Ta-ti-tup!' echoed a fanfare.

The sound of rattles was something like applause.

'Lapitup the strongman will demonstrate for you the wonders of his strength…'

The band crashed out. The curtain opened. Out onto the stage came Lapitup the strongman.

This huge fellow in a pink leotard did, indeed, seem very strong.

He was breathing heavily through his nose and bowing his head like a bull. The muscles moved beneath his skin like rabbits swallowed by a boa constrictor.

Assistants brought some weights and dropped them onto the stage. The boards almost gave way. A column of dust and sawdust flew up. A buzz went round the whole market.

The strongman began displaying his art. He took a weight in each hand, threw them up into the air like little balls, caught them, and then swung them against one another with a crash... Sparks flew.

'There!' he said. 'That's the way the Three Fat Men will smash the foreheads of Prospero the armourer and Tibullus the acrobat.'

The strongman too had been won over by the gold of the Three Fat Men.

'Ha-ha-ha!' he thundered, pleased with his joke.

He knew no one would risk flinging a flat cake at him. Everyone could see his strength.

In the silence that fell, the voice of the black man rang out distinctly. An entire kitchen garden of heads turned in his direction.

'What's that you're saying?' the black man asked, setting one foot on the first step.

'I'm saying that that's the way, forehead to forehead, the Three Fat Men will crush the heads of Prospero the armourer and Tibullus the acrobat.'

'Shut up!'

The black man spoke calmly, sternly and quietly.

'And who are you, you black scum?' said the strongman angrily.

He dropped the weights and put his hands on his hips.

The black man went up onto the stage.

'You're very strong, but no less vile. Better, you tell me who you are. Who gave you the right to scoff at the people? I know you. You're a hammerman's son. Your father works in a factory to this day. Your sister's name is Ellie. She's a laundress. She washes rich men's linen. She may have been shot by the guardsmen yesterday. And you're a traitor!'

The strongman took a step back in amazement. What the black man had said was, indeed, the truth. The strongman couldn't understand a thing.

'Get out of here!' cried the black man.

The strongman recovered himself. His face became blood-shot. He clenched his fists.

'You have no right to give me orders!' he said with difficulty. 'I don't know you. You're a demon.'

'Get out of here! I shall count to three. One!'

The crowd froze. The black man was a head shorter than Lapitup and three times as slim, yet nobody doubted that, in the event of a fight, the black man would win, so decisive, stern and confident was his air.

'Two!'

The strongman drew his head in.

'You devil!' he hissed.

'Three!'

The strongman vanished. A lot of people had screwed up their eyes, expecting a terrible blow, and when they opened them, the strongman was no longer there. In an instant he had vanished behind a screen.

'And that's the way the people will drive out the Three Fat Men,' the black man said merrily, raising his arms.

The crowd was tempestuous in its delight. People clapped their hands and threw their hats into the air.

'Long live the people!'

'Bravo! Bravo!'

Only Dr Gaspar was shaking his head discontentedly. What he was discontented about, no one knows.

'Who is he? Who is he! Who is this black man?' wondered the spectators.

'Is he an actor too?'

'We've never seen him before!'

'Who are you?'

'Why did you come out in our defence?'

'Excuse me! Excuse me!'

Some sort of ragamuffin pushed his way through the crowd. It was the same beggar who had been talking the previous evening with the flower-sellers and the coachmen. Dr Gaspar recognised him.

'Excuse me!' said the beggar in agitation. 'Can't you see we're being tricked? This black man is just as much an actor as Lapitup the strongman. The same gang. He's had money from the Three Fat Men too.'

The black man clenched his fists.

The crowd's delight turned to anger:

'Of course! One good-for-nothing's been driven away by another.'

'He was afraid we'd give his comrade a beating, and he's pulled a fast one.'

'Down with him!'

'The good-for-nothing!'

'The traitor!'

Dr Gaspar tried to say something, to restrain the crowd, but it was too late. A dozen or so men had run up onto the stage and surrounded the black man.

'Hit him!' shrieked an old woman.

The black man reached out an arm. He was calm.

'Stop!'

His voice rose above the cries, the noise and the whistles. It became quiet, and in the quietness the black man's words rang out calmly and simply:

'I am Tibullus the acrobat.'

There was confusion.

The ring of assailants fell back.

'Ah!' the crowd sighed.

Hundreds of people gave a start, then froze.

And just one person asked in perplexity:

'But why are you black?'

'Ask Dr Gaspar Arneri about that.' And with a smile, the black man pointed to the doctor.

'It's him, of course it is!'

'Tibullus!'

'Hurrah! Tibullus is safe! Tibullus is alive! Tibullus is with us!'

'Long live…'

But the cry stopped short. Something unforeseen and unpleasant had happened. The people at the back of the crowd were in confusion. People were scattering in all directions.

'Quiet! Quiet!'

'Run, Tibullus, try and get away!'

Three horsemen and a carriage had appeared in the square.

It was the Captain of the Palace Guard, Count Bonaventura, accompanied by two guardsmen. In the carriage rode the palace official with the broken doll of Tutti the Heir. Its wonderful little head with its curls cut short was nestling sadly against his shoulder.

They were looking for Dr Gaspar.

'Guardsmen!' somebody yelled at the top of his voice.

Several people leapt over a fence.

The black carriage stopped. The horses shook their heads. The harness jingled and glittered. The wind ruffled the blue feathers.

The horsemen surrounded the carriage.

Captain Bonaventura had an awful voice. If that fiddle gave you toothache, this voice gave you the feeling of having had a tooth knocked out.

He rose in his stirrups and asked:

'Where is the house of Dr Gaspar Arneri?'

He was pulling on the reins. On his hands he had rough leather gloves with widely flared mouths.

This question fell like ball lightning upon an old woman who waved a hand in fright in an indefinite direction.

'Where?' the Captain repeated.

The sound of his voice now was enough for it to seem as though not one tooth had been knocked out, but a whole jawful.

'I'm here. Who's asking for me?'

People stepped aside. Treading carefully, Dr Gaspar passed through to the carriage.

'Are you Dr Gaspar Arneri?'

'I am Dr Gaspar Arneri.'

The carriage door opened.

'Get into the carriage at once. You'll be taken to your house, and there you'll find out what it's all about.'

A groom leapt down from the footboard at the back of the carriage and helped the doctor in. The door slammed shut.

The cavalcade moved off, ploughing up the dry earth. A minute later they had all disappeared around a corner.

Neither Captain Bonaventura nor the guardsmen had seen Tibullus the acrobat at the back of the crowd. If they had seen the black man, they probably wouldn't have recognised in him the man they had been hunting the night before.

The danger seemed to have passed. But suddenly a malevolent hissing was heard.

Lapitup the strongman had poked his head out from behind the calico-covered barrier and was hissing:

'Just you wait... just you wait, pal!' He threatened Tibullus with his enormous great fist: 'Just you wait, I'm going to catch up with the guardsmen and tell them you're here!'

With these words he started climbing over the barrier. The barrier couldn't take the weight of the pink hulk. With a duck-like quack, the barrier broke.

The strongman pulled his leg through the gap that had been formed and, pushing the knot of people aside, he started running after the carriage.

'Stop!' he howled as he went, waving his rounded, bare arms. 'Stop! Tibullus the acrobat's been found! Tibullus the acrobat's here! He's in my hands!'

Things were taking a menacing turn. And at this point the Spaniard with the rolling eye got involved too; he had a pistol in his belt and he held another pistol in his hand. The Spaniard kicked up a racket. He jumped up and down on the stage, shouting out:

'Citizens! We have to give Tibullus up to the guardsmen, otherwise things will go badly for us. Citizens, we mustn't quarrel with the Three Fat Men!'

He was joined by the owner of the booth in which Lapitup the strongman had given such an unfortunate performance.

'He ruined my show! He got rid of Lapitup the strongman! I don't want to be answerable to the Three Fat Men for him!'

The crowd formed a protective wall around Tibullus.

The strongman was unable to catch up with the guardsmen. He reappeared in the square. He was rushing at full speed straight at Tibullus. The Spaniard leapt down from the stage and pulled out the second pistol. From somewhere the owner of the booth produced a hoop of white paper – one of those that trained dogs jump through in the circus. He was waving the hoop around and hobbling down from the stage after the Spaniard.

The Spaniard cocked his pistol.

Tibullus saw that he had to flee. The crowd made way. The next moment Tibullus was no longer in the square. Jumping over a fence, he found himself in a kitchen garden. He looked through a gap in the fence. The strongman, the Spaniard and the showman were running towards the kitchen garden. It was a very funny sight. Tibullus laughed. The strongman was running like an enraged elephant, the Spaniard looked like a rat, hopping along on its hind legs, while the showman was limping like a wounded crow.

'We're going to take you alive!' they cried. 'Surrender!'

The Spaniard was clicking the cocking-piece and his teeth. The showman was shaking the paper hoop.

Tibullus waited for the attack. He was standing on loose black earth. All around him were beds of vegetables. There were cabbages and beetroots growing here, green runners of some sort were winding about, stalks were poking up, and broad leaves were lying around.

Everything was stirring in the wind. The clear blue sky was shining brightly.

The battle began.

All three men approached the fence.

'Are you there?' asked the strongman.

No one answered.

Then the Spaniard said:

'Surrender! I've got a pistol in each hand. The pistols are the very best make – "Scoundrel & Son". I'm the best shot in the country, do you understand?'

Tibullus didn't excel in the art of pistol-shooting. He didn't even have a pistol, but he did have to hand, or rather, to foot, a very large number of cabbages. He bent down and picked one, round and weighty, and flung it over the fence. The cabbage hit the showman in the stomach. Then a second one went flying, and a third. They exploded no worse than bombs.

The enemy was bewildered.

Tibullus bent down for a fourth. He seized it by its round cheeks and strained to pull it up, but – alas! – the cabbage wouldn't yield. What's more, it started speaking in a human voice:

'This isn't a head of cabbage, it's *my* head. I'm the children's balloon seller. I was escaping from the Three Fat Men's palace and found myself in an underground passage. It starts in a saucepan and it ends here. It runs under the ground like a long intestine...'

Tibullus couldn't believe his ears: a head of cabbage was passing itself off as a human one!

Then he bent down and had a look at this wonder. He had to believe his eyes. The eyes of a man who can walk a tightrope don't lie.

What he saw did, indeed, have nothing in common with a head of cabbage. It was the round face of the balloon seller. As always, it looked like a teapot – a narrow-spouted teapot, decorated with daisies.

The balloon seller was looking out of the ground, and the churned-up earth, which was scattered about him in damp clods, ringed his neck like a black collar.

'Hello!' said Tibullus.

The balloon seller looked at him with round eyes, in which was reflected the tender sky.

'I gave my balloons away to the kitchen boys, and the kitchen boys released me... And there goes one of the balloons, by the way...'

Tibullus looked, and ever so high up in the dazzling blue he saw a small orange balloon.

It was one of the balloons released by the kitchen-lads.

The trio standing on the other side of the fence and thinking over their plan of attack saw the balloon as well. The Spaniard forgot about everything. The Spaniard jumped seven feet up in the air, rolled his other eye and took up his position. He was passionate about shooting.

'Look,' he cried, 'there's an idiotic balloon at a height of ten bell-towers. I bet ten gold pieces I can hit it. There's no better shot than me.'

Nobody wanted to have a bet with him, but that didn't cool

the Spaniard down. The strongman and the showman became indignant.

'You ass!' growled the strongman. 'You ass! This is no time for hunting balloons! You ass! We've got to capture Tibullus. Don't waste your cartridges.'

Nothing was of any use. The balloon seemed too enticing a target for the crack shot. The Spaniard began to take aim, closing his irrepressible eye. And while he was aiming, Tibullus pulled the balloon seller out of the ground. What a sight he was! The things that were on his clothes! The remains of the butter cream and syrup, and bits of earth that had got stuck on, and delicate little stars of candied peel!

A black hole was left in the spot from which Tibullus had pulled him like a cork from a bottle. Earth sprinkled down into the hole, and the resultant sound was just like big drops of rain pounding on the raised hood of a carriage.

The Spaniard fired. Of course, he didn't hit the balloon. But alas, he did hit the showman's green hat, which was itself the height of one bell-tower.

Tibullus escaped from the kitchen garden by jumping over the opposite fence.

The green hat fell and rolled away like a samovar's smoke-stack. The Spaniard was terribly embarrassed: his reputation as the best shot had been lost! What's more, the showman's respect had been lost too.

'Oh, you good-for-nothing!' The showman was beside himself and, choking with rage, he swung the paper hoop down onto the Spaniard's head.

It tore apart with a snap, and the Spaniard's head found itself in a jagged paper collar.

Only Lapitup was left doing nothing. But the shot had alarmed the neighbourhood's dogs. One of them flew out from somewhere and went hurtling towards the strongman.

'Every man for himself!' Lapitup had time to cry.

All three took flight.

The balloon seller alone remained. He clambered up onto the fence and looked around. The three pals had gone tumbling down a green slope. Lapitup was hopping on one leg, clutching his fat calf, which had been bitten; the showman had climbed a tree, and was hanging there looking like an owl; and the Spaniard was waggling his head, which was still poking out of the paper hoop, and trying to fend off the dog by shooting, hitting the kitchen garden's scarecrow every time.

The dog was standing at the top of the slope and evidently had no desire to attack again. Completely satisfied by the taste of Lapitup's calf, it was wagging its tail and smiling broadly with its glossy pink tongue hanging out.

Something Unforeseen

'Ask Dr Gaspar Arneri,' Tibullus the acrobat had replied to the question why he had become a black man.

But even without asking Dr Gaspar, the reason can be guessed. Let's remember: Tibullus had managed to escape from the battlefield. Let's remember: the guardsmen were hunting for him, they were setting fire to the workers' districts, they had opened fire in Star Circus. Tibullus had found refuge in Dr Gaspar's house. But even there he could have been found at any moment. The danger was obvious. Too many people knew what he looked like.

All the shopkeepers were on the side of the Three Fat Men, because they themselves were fat and rich. Any of the rich men living in Dr Gaspar's neighbourhood might inform the guardsmen that the doctor had given Tibullus shelter.

'You need to alter your appearance,' Dr Gaspar had said in the night, when Tibullus had come to his house.

And Dr Gaspar had made Tibullus different.

He had said:

'You're a giant. You have an enormous chest, wide shoulders, gleaming teeth, curly, wiry black hair. If it weren't for your white skin, you'd look like a North American negro. Excellent! I'll help you to become black.'

Dr Gaspar Arneri had studied a hundred branches of learning. He was a very serious man, but he had a genial nature. All work and no play make Jack a dull boy. And sometimes he liked to enjoy himself. But even when relaxing, he remained a scholar. At such times he would prepare transfers as presents for the poor children in orphanages, create amazing fireworks and toys, make musical instruments with voices of unprecedented charm, mix new shades of paint.

'Now,' he had said to Tibullus, 'now look. In *this* flask there's a colourless liquid. But when it comes into contact with any body, reacting with dry air, it stains the body black, moreover, precisely the purplish sort of tint that is characteristic of the black man. And in *this* flask is an essence which nullifies the stain.'

Tibullus had taken off his leotard, fashioned out of different coloured triangles, and had rubbed himself with the stinging liquid that smelt of burning.

An hour later he had become black.

At that point Auntie Ganymede had come in with her mouse. The rest we know.

Let us return to Dr Gaspar. We parted with him at the moment when Captain Bonaventura took him away in the palace official's black carriage.

The carriage flew along at top speed. We already know that Lapitup the strongman couldn't catch up with it.

It was dark in the carriage. When he found himself inside, the doctor decided at first that the official sitting next to him was holding a child on his lap – a little girl whose hair was dishevelled.

The official was silent. The child too.

'Forgive me, have I taken up too much room?' asked the polite doctor, raising his hat.

The official replied dryly:

'Don't trouble yourself.'

Light came fleetingly through the narrow windows of the carriage. After a minute, the doctor's eyes had become accustomed to the darkness, and then he made out the long nose and half-lowered eyelids of the official and the delightful little girl in her smart dress. The girl seemed very sad. And she was probably pale, though this couldn't be determined in the gloom.

'The poor little thing,' thought Dr Gaspar. 'She must be ill.'

And he turned once more to the official:

'In all probability my assistance is required? The poor child's fallen ill?'

'Yes, your assistance is required,' replied the official with the long nose.

'No doubt this is a niece of one of the Three Fat Men, or a little guest of Tutti the Heir,' the doctor reasoned to himself. 'She's richly dressed, she's been brought from the palace, the Captain of the Guard is accompanying her – she's clearly a very important person. Yes, but living children aren't allowed near Tutti the Heir, are they? How ever did this little angel get into the palace?'

The doctor was lost in conjecture. Again he tried to strike up a conversation with the big-nosed official:

'Tell me, what's the matter with the little girl? Not diphtheria, is it?'

'No, it's a hole in the chest.'

'Do you mean she has something wrong with her lungs?'

'It's a hole in the chest,' the official repeated.

Out of politeness, the doctor didn't argue.

'The poor little girl!' he sighed.

'It's not a girl, it's a doll,' said the official.

At this point the carriage drove up to the doctor's house.

The official with the doll and Captain Bonaventura followed the doctor into the house. The doctor received them in the workshop.

'If it's a doll, then why might my services be needed?'

The official began to explain, and everything became clear.

Auntie Ganymede, who had still not recovered from the excitements of the morning, was peeping through the keyhole. She could see the terrifying Captain Bonaventura. He stood leaning on his sabre and occasionally wiggling his foot in its huge boot with the top folded down. His spurs looked like comets. Auntie could see a sad, sick little girl in a smart pink dress, who had been sat down in an armchair by the official. The girl had let her head with its tousled hair droop, and seemed to be looking down at her sweet little feet in satin slippers which had gold roses instead of pompons.

The strong wind was tossing the gallery shutter to and fro, and the banging made it hard for Auntie Ganymede to listen.

But she did understand a certain amount.

The official showed Dr Gaspar the order from the State Council of the Three Fat Men. The doctor read it and became agitated.

'The doll must be repaired by tomorrow morning,' said the official, getting up.

Captain Bonaventura jangled his spurs.

'Yes... but...' the doctor spread his hands. 'I'll try, but can I give a guarantee? I'm unfamiliar with this magical doll's mechanism. I need to study it, I need to establish the nature of the injuries, I need to manufacture the new parts of the mechanism.

That will require a great deal of time. Perhaps my art will prove powerless… Perhaps I won't succeed in restoring the health of the wounded doll… I'm afraid, gentlemen… Such a short time… Only one night… I can't promise…'

The official cut him short. Raising a finger, he said,

'Tutti the Heir's grief is too great for us to be able to delay. The doll must revive by tomorrow morning. Such is the will of the Three Fat Men. No one dares disobey their order. Tomorrow morning you will bring the repaired, healthy doll to the Palace of the Three Fat Men.'

'Yes… but…' protested the doctor.

'No arguments! The doll must be repaired by tomorrow morning. If you do it, then a reward awaits you, if not – then a severe punishment.'

The doctor was stunned.

'I'll try,' he babbled. 'But you must understand, it's too responsible a matter…'

'Of course,' the official snapped, and he lowered his finger. 'I've given you the order, and it's your duty to carry it out. Farewell!…'

Auntie Ganymede sprang back from the door and ran off to her room, where the fortunate mouse was eating greedily in a corner. The terrifying guests left the house. The official got into the carriage; Count Bonaventura, with a flashing and a jingling, leapt onto his horse; the guardsmen pulled their hats down, and everyone galloped off.

Tutti the Heir's doll remained in the doctor's workshop.

The doctor saw his guests off, then sought out Auntie Ganymede and said to her in an unusually stern voice,

'Auntie Ganymede! Remember this. I value my reputation for being a wise man, an accomplished doctor and a skilled craftsman. And apart from that, I value my head. Tomorrow morning I may lose both the one and the other. Difficult work lies ahead of me the whole night long. Do you understand?' He waved the order from the State Council of the Three Fat Men. 'No one must disturb me. Make no noise. Don't make a clatter with the plates. Don't cause a fug. Don't call the hens. Don't catch any mice. No scrambled eggs, cauliflower, fruit jelly or valerian drops! Do you understand?'

Dr Gaspar was very angry.

Auntie Ganymede locked herself in her room.

'Strange goings-on, very strange goings-on!' she grumbled. 'I don't understand a thing. Some sort of black man, some sort of doll, some sort of order… Strange days are upon us!'

To calm herself down, she decided to write a letter to her niece. She had to write very carefully so that the pen didn't scratch. She was afraid of disturbing the doctor.

An hour went by. Auntie Ganymede kept on writing. She got to a description of the astonishing black man who had appeared that morning in Dr Gaspar's workshop.

They went off together. The doctor came back with a palace official and some guardsmen. They brought a doll that couldn't be told apart from a little girl, but the black man wasn't with them. Where he's got to, I don't know…

The question of where the black man, otherwise Tibullus the acrobat, had got to was worrying Dr Gaspar too. As he worked on the doll, he didn't stop thinking about Tibullus' fate. He got angry. He talked to himself:

'What indiscretion! I'd turned him into a black man and stained him a wonderful colour, I'd made him completely unrecognisable, then today he went and gave himself away at the Fourteenth Market. I mean, he could be captured… Ah! How indiscreet he is! He doesn't want to end up in an iron cage, does he?'

Dr Gaspar was greatly upset. Tibullus' indiscretion, and then this doll... And apart from that, the troubles of the previous day, the ten scaffolds in Court Square...

'A terrible time!' exclaimed the doctor.

He didn't know that the execution due that day had been cancelled. The palace official hadn't been talkative. He hadn't told the doctor about what had happened that day at the palace.

The doctor examined the poor doll and wondered:

'Where have these wounds come from? They've been inflicted by cold steel, probably a sabre. The doll, the wonderful little girl, was stabbed again and again... Who did it? Who dared to stab Tutti the Heir's doll with a sabre?'

The doctor didn't suppose that it was guardsmen who had done it. He couldn't have had any idea that even the Palace Guard was refusing to serve the Three Fat Men and was going over to the side of the people. How he would have rejoiced if he had learnt of it!

The doctor took the doll's head in his hands. The sunlight was flying in through the window. It lit the doll up brightly. The doctor looked.

'Strange, very strange,' he mused. 'I've seen this face before somewhere... Well yes, of course I have! I have seen it, I recognise it. But where? When? It was alive, it was the living face of a little girl, it was smiling, pulling lovely little faces, it was attentive, it was coquettish and sad... Yes, yes. There can be no doubt about it! But my accursed myopia prevents me from remembering faces!'

He brought the doll's curly head up close to his eyes.

'What an amazing doll! What a clever craftsman created it! It's not like an ordinary doll. A doll usually has wide-open, bright-blue eyes, inhuman and expressionless, a little turned-up nose, a Cupid's bow, silly blond curls exactly like a lamb's. A doll appears to look happy, but in reality it's stupid… Yet there's nothing doll-like about this doll. I swear it might seem like a little girl who's turned into a doll!'

Dr Gaspar feasted his eyes upon his extraordinary patient. And all the time the idea never abandoned him that somewhere, sometime, he had seen this same pale face, the attentive grey eyes, the short, tousled hair. The turn of the head and the gaze seemed particularly familiar to him: it inclined its head a little to one side and looked at the doctor from below, attentively, mischievously…

The doctor couldn't contain himself and asked loudly,

'What's your name, doll?'

But the girl was silent. Then the doctor suddenly remembered. The doll was damaged; he had to give her back her voice, mend her heart, teach her to smile again, to dance and behave the way girls of her age do.

'To look at, she's twelve.'

He couldn't delay. The doctor set about the work. 'I have to revive the doll.'

Auntie Ganymede had finished writing her letter. She had been bored for two hours. Then she had become filled with curiosity. 'What's the urgent work Dr Gaspar has to carry out? What is this doll?'

She stole up quietly to the doors of the workshop and glanced into the heart-shaped keyhole. Alas! The key had been put into it! She saw nothing, but then the door opened, and out came Dr Gaspar. He was so upset that he didn't even reprimand Auntie Ganymede for her indiscretion. But Auntie Ganymede was embarrassed enough as it was.

'Auntie Ganymede,' said the doctor. 'I'm leaving. Or rather, I have to go. Summon a cab.'

He paused, and then began rubbing his forehead with the palm of his hand.

'I'm going to the Palace of the Three Fat Men. It's highly likely that I won't be coming back.'

Auntie Ganymede took a step back in amazement.

'To the Palace of the Three Fat Men?'

'Yes, Auntie Ganymede. It's a very nasty business. They brought me Tutti the Heir's doll. It's the best doll in the world. Its mechanism's broken. The State Council of the Three Fat Men ordered me to repair the doll by tomorrow morning. I'm threatened with severe punishment.'

Auntie Ganymede was getting ready to burst into tears.

'And it turns out I can't repair the poor doll. I've taken the mechanism hidden in its chest apart, I understand its secret, I would have been able to restore it. But... such a little thing! Because of a trifle, Auntie Ganymede, I can't do it. There, in that cunning mechanism, there's a cogwheel – it's cracked... It's no good at all! A new one needs to be made... I have a suitable metal, like silver... But before you can start work, the metal needs to be kept in a vitriol solution for at least two days. You understand, two days... And the doll has to be ready tomorrow morning.'

'And can't you put in some other wheel?' Auntie Ganymede suggested timidly.

The doctor waved his hand sadly.

'I've tried everything, nothing works.'

Five minutes later, in front of Dr Gaspar's house there stood a covered cab. The doctor had decided to go to the Palace of the Three Fat Men.

'I'll tell them that the doll can't be ready by tomorrow morning. Let them do with me what they will...'

Auntie Ganymede bit her apron and shook her head until she was scared that her head would drop off.

Dr Gaspar sat the doll down beside him and drove away.

The Night of the Strange Doll

The wind was whistling into both of Dr Gaspar's ears. The resulting melody was repellent, even worse than the negro galop duet that a grinding wheel and knife rattle out in the hands of a diligent grinder.

The doctor covered his ears with his collar and presented his back to the wind.

Then the wind started on the stars. First it would blow them out, then roll them around, and then knock them down behind the black triangles of roofs. When it was tired of that game, it thought of the clouds. But the clouds collapsed like towers. All at once at that point the wind became cold: it turned cold out of spite.

The doctor had to wrap himself in his cape. Half of the cape he gave up to the doll.

'Drive faster! Drive faster! Please, drive faster!'

For no apparent reason, the doctor had begun to feel scared, and he hurried the coachman along.

It was very ominous, dark and desolate. Only in a few windows did little reddish lights appear, the rest had their shutters closed. People were expecting terrible events.

There was a lot that seemed unusual and suspicious that evening. And at times the doctor was even afraid that the strange doll's eyes might start shining in the darkness like two transparent stones. He tried not to look at his travelling companion.

'Nonsense!' he tried to reassure himself. 'My nerves are frazzled. It's the most ordinary evening. It's just that there aren't many passers-by. It's just that the wind is throwing their shadows about so strangely that everyone we do meet seems like a hired killer in a mysterious winged cape... It's just that the gas lamps at the crossroads are burning with a sort of deathly blue light... Oh, if only we could get to the Palace of the Three Fat Men quickly!...'

There is one very good remedy for fear: falling asleep. Particularly recommended is pulling a blanket over your head. The doctor resorted to this remedy. For the blanket he substituted his hat, which he pulled down tight over his eyes. Well, and, of course, he started counting to a hundred. It didn't help. Then he used a powerful remedy. He repeated to himself:

'One elephant and one elephant is two elephants; two elephants and one elephant is three elephants; three elephants and one elephant is four elephants...'

It got to the point of a whole herd of elephants. And it was the one hundred and twenty-third elephant that turned from an imaginary elephant into a real one. And since the doctor couldn't make out whether it was an elephant or the pink strongman Lapitup, the doctor was evidently asleep and starting to dream.

Time passes much quicker in a dream than in reality. At least, in his dream the doctor had time not only to reach the Palace of the Three Fat Men, but also to appear in their court. Each of them stood before him holding a doll by the hand, the way a Gypsy holds his blue-skirted monkey.

They didn't want to hear any explanations.

'You've failed to carry out an order,' they said. 'You deserve a severe punishment. You're to walk the high wire above Star Circus with the doll. Only take your glasses off...'

The doctor begged forgiveness. He was mainly afraid for the fate of the doll... This is what he said:

'I'm already used to it, I already know about falling down... If I come off the wire and fall into the pool, that's quite all right. I have experience: I fell down with the tower in the square by the town gates... But the doll, the poor doll! She'll be smashed to smithereens... Have pity on her... I'm certain she's not a doll, you know, but a living girl with a wonderful name which I've forgotten, which I can't remember...'

'No!' cried the Fat Men. 'No! No forgiveness! It's by order of the Three Fat Men!'

The cry was so harsh that the doctor woke up.

'It's by order of the Three Fat Men!' someone was shouting right in his ear.

The doctor was no longer asleep now. This shouting was in real life. The doctor freed his eyes, or rather, his glasses from beneath his hat and looked around. While he had been asleep, the night had had time to become decidedly black.

The carriage was standing still. It was surrounded by black figures: it was they who had started the shouting and got mixed up in the doctor's dream. They were waving lanterns around. As a result there were latticed shadows flying about.

'What's going on?' asked the doctor. 'Where are we? Who are these people?'

One of the figures approached and raised a lantern to head height, throwing light onto the doctor. The lantern started swaying. The hand which held it by a ring from above was in a glove of rough leather with a widely flared mouth.

The doctor understood: guardsmen.

'It's by order of the Three Fat Men,' the figure repeated.

The yellow light broke the figure up into pieces. Its oilskin hat glimmered, and in the night-time gave the impression it was made of iron.

'No one has the right to come closer than a kilometre to the palace. The order was issued today. There are disturbances in town. You can't go any further.'

'Yes, but it's essential I present myself at the palace.'

The doctor was indignant.

The guardsman spoke in a voice of iron:

'I'm the officer of the watch, Captain Reppep. I won't let you go a single step further. Turn around!' he cried to the coachman, waving the lantern at him.

The doctor became uneasy. He was in no doubt, however, that upon learning who he was and why he needed to go to the palace, they would let him pass at once.

'I'm Dr Gaspar Arneri,' he said.

In reply there was a roar of laughter. On all sides the lanterns started dancing.

'Citizen, we're not inclined to joke at such a troubled time and at such a late hour,' said the officer of the watch.

'I repeat, I am Dr Gaspar Arneri.'

The officer of the watch flew into a fury. Slowly and clearly, accompanying each word with a clang of his sabre, he said,

'In order to get into the palace you are using another man's name as cover. Dr Gaspar Arneri does not roam around at night. Especially *this* night. He is now engaged in the most important work: he is reviving the doll of Tutti the Heir. Only tomorrow morning will he present himself at the palace. And you, as an impostor, are under arrest.'

'What?!' Now it was the doctor who was furious.

'What?!' he thought. 'Does he dare not to believe me? Very well. Now I'll show him the doll!'

The doctor reached his arm out for the doll – and suddenly…

The doll wasn't there. It had fallen out of the carriage while he was asleep.

The doctor turned cold.

'Perhaps this is still a dream?' flashed through his mind.

Alas! It was reality.

'Well!' muttered the office of the watch, gritting his teeth and flexing the fingers that held the lantern. 'Get the hell out of here! I'm letting you go because I can't be bothered with a wretched old man… Go away!'

He had to be obeyed. The coachman turned around. The carriage creaked, the horse snorted, the iron lanterns swung one last time, and the poor doctor started back again.

He couldn't contain himself and burst into tears. He had been spoken to so rudely, he had been called a wretched old man, and, most important of all – he had lost Tutti the Heir's doll!

'And that means I've lost my head in the most literal sense.'

He cried. His glasses steamed up, he couldn't see a thing. He felt like burying his head in a pillow. In the meantime, the coachman was driving the horse on. The doctor was distressed for ten minutes. But soon his usual good sense returned to him.

'I may still be able to find the doll,' he considered. 'There aren't many passers-by tonight. This is always a desolate spot. It may well be that nobody has gone down the road in all this time…'

He ordered the coachman to proceed at a walk and to examine the road carefully.

'Well? Well?' he asked every minute.

'Nothing to be seen. Nothing to be seen,' replied the coachman.

He reported quite unnecessary and uninteresting finds.

'A small barrel.'

'No… that's not it…'

'A good, large sheet of glass.'

'No.'

'A ripped shoe.'

'No,' the doctor replied ever more quietly.

The coachman tried his hardest. He tired his eyes out looking. He saw so well in the dark, it was as if he weren't a coachman, but the captain of an ocean-going ship.

'A doll, can't you see a doll, though? A doll in a pink dress?'

'There's no doll,' said the coachman in a sad bass voice.

'Well, in that case it's been picked up. There's no point in looking any more… It was here, at this spot, I fell asleep… It was still sitting next to me then… Oh dear!…'

And the doctor was ready to burst into tears again.

The coachman sniffed several times in sympathy.

'What's to be done?'

'Oh, I just don't know... Oh, I just don't know...' The doctor sat with his head in his hands, rocking to and fro in grief, and also at the bumping of the carriage. 'I know,' he said. 'But of course... but of course... Why didn't it occur to me before! It ran away, the doll! I fell asleep and it ran away. It's obvious. It was a living doll. I could see it at once. However, that doesn't make me any less guilty in the eyes of the Three Fat Men...'

At this point he felt like something to eat. He was silent for a while, and then he announced very grandly:

'I didn't have any dinner today. Take me to the nearest inn.'

Hunger calmed the doctor down.

They drove for a long time down dark streets. All the inn-keepers had closed their doors. All the fat people were going through some anxious hours that night.

They had nailed up new bolts and barricaded their entrances with chests of drawers and wardrobes. They had stopped the windows with mattresses and striped pillows. They weren't asleep. Everyone who was on the fat and rich side was expecting to be attacked that night. Watchdogs hadn't been fed since morning to make them more alert and fierce. A terrible night had arrived for the rich and fat. They were certain that at any minute the people might rise up once again. A rumour that some guardsmen had betrayed the Three Fat Men, had stabbed Tutti the Heir's doll and left the palace had spread through the town. This was very alarming for all the rich people and the gluttons.

'Damn it!' they fumed. 'We can't rely on the guardsmen any more. Yesterday they suppressed the people's revolt, and today they'll be aiming their cannon at our houses.'

Dr Gaspar lost all hope of satisfying his hunger and having a rest. There were no signs of life around anywhere.

'Must I really go home?' implored the doctor. 'But it's such a long way. I'll die of hunger.'

Then he suddenly smelt roast meat. Yes, there was a pleasant smell of roasting food: probably lamb and onions. And at the same moment, the coachman caught sight of a light not far away. There was a narrow strip of light swaying in the wind.

What was it?

'If only it could be an inn!' exclaimed the doctor in delight.

They drove up.

It proved not to be an inn at all.

On some wasteland, at a distance from a few cottages, there stood a house on wheels.

The narrow strip of light proved to be a crack in the house's door, which wasn't fully closed.

The coachman climbed down from his box and went on a recce. The doctor, forgetting his misadventures, revelled in the smell of the roast meat. He breathed deeply, whistling through his nose, and screwed his eyes up tight.

'Firstly, I'm scared of dogs!' shouted the coachman from the darkness. 'Secondly, there are steps of some sort over here…'

Everything turned out all right. The coachman clambered up the steps to the doors and knocked.

'Who's there?'

The narrow strip of light turned into a broad, bright rectangle. The door opened wide. On the threshold stood a man. Amidst the surrounding empty gloom and against the brightly lit background he seemed flat, like a black paper cut-out.

The coachman replied on behalf of the doctor:

'It's Dr Gaspar Arneri. And who are you? Whose is this house on wheels?'

'This here's Uncle Brizak's travelling show,' replied the Chinese shadow from the threshold. It was pleased about something, it got excited and started waving its arms about. 'This way, gentlemen, this way! We're very glad that Dr Gaspar Arneri has come to visit Uncle Brizak's travelling show.'

A happy ending! Enough of nocturnal wanderings! Long live Uncle Brizak's travelling show!

The doctor, the coachman and the horse had found refuge, dinner, rest. The house on wheels proved a hospitable one. In it lived Uncle Brizak's roving troupe.

Who hadn't heard that name! Who didn't know of Uncle Brizak's travelling show! All year round on holidays and fair-days the show put on its performances in market squares. What skilled actors there were here! How gripping their shows were! And the main thing was, it was here, in this travelling show, that the tightrope walker Tibullus performed.

We already know he had covered himself in glory as the best tightrope walker in the land. We were witnesses to his agility in Star Circus, when he walked the wire over a terrifying abyss under a hail of bullets from the guardsmen.

How many blisters popped up on the hands of spectators both large and small, when Tibullus performed in market squares – so enthusiastically was he clapped by shopkeepers, old beggar-women, schoolchildren, soldiers, by everyone, everyone... Now, though, the shopkeepers and dandies regretted their former rapture: 'We used to applaud him, but now he's fighting against us!'

Uncle Brizak's travelling show was orphaned: Tibullus the acrobat had abandoned it.

Dr Gaspar said nothing about what had happened to Tibullus. He also kept quiet about Tutti the Heir's doll.

What did the doctor see in the wagon, inside the house on wheels?

He was given a seat on a large Turkish drum, decorated with crimson triangles and gold wire woven in the form of a net. The house, built in the manner of a railway carriage, consisted of several sets of quarters, separated by canvas partitions.

The hour was late. The population of the wagon was asleep. The man who had opened the door and seemed to be a Chinese shadow was none other than the old clown. His name was Augustus. Tonight he was on watch. When the doctor had driven up to the booth, Augustus had been preparing his dinner. It was, indeed, lamb with onions.

The doctor sat on the drum and examined his surroundings. A paraffin lamp was burning on a crate. On the walls hung hoops with white and pink rice-paper stretched onto them, long striped whips with shiny metal handles, costumes sprinkled with little gold circles, embroidered with flowers, stars and multi-coloured scraps of material. From the walls gazed masks. Some had horns sticking out; on others the noses were like Turkish slippers; on still others the mouths went from ear to ear. One mask was notable for its enormous ears. The funniest thing was that the ears were human ones, only very big.

In a corner, in a cage, sat some peculiar little animal. By one of the walls was a long, wooden table. Above it hung some little mirrors. Ten of them. Next to each mirror stood a candle, stuck to the table by its own juice, its stearin. The candles weren't lit. Scattered on the table were little boxes, brushes, paints, powder-puffs and wigs, there was pink powder lying about, and little multi-coloured pools of liquid were drying up.

'We spent today getting away from the guardsmen,' began the clown. 'You know that Tibullus the acrobat was one of our actors. The guardsmen wanted to seize us: they think we've hidden him.'

The old clown seemed very sad.

'But we don't know ourselves where Tibullus the acrobat is. He must have been killed or put in an iron cage.'

The clown was sighing, and shaking his grey head. The animal in the cage was looking at the doctor with feline eyes.

'It's a pity you've come to us so late,' said the clown. 'We're very fond of you. You would have reassured us. We know you're a friend of the deprived, a friend of the people. I'll remind you of one occasion. We were giving a show at the Ox Liver Market. It was last year in the spring. My little girl sang a song...'

'Right, right...' the doctor tried to recall. Suddenly he felt a strange excitement.

'Remember? You were at the market at the time. You watched our performance. My little girl sang a song about a pie which preferred to burn in the oven rather than end up in the stomach of a fat nobleman...'

'Yes, yes... I do remember... Go on!'

'A grand lady, an old woman, heard it and took offence. She ordered her big-nosed servants to box my little girl's ears.'

'Yes, I remember. I intervened. I sent the servants packing. The lady recognised me and was ashamed of herself. Correct?'

'Yes. Then you left, and my little girl said that if the grand old woman's servants had boxed her ears, she wouldn't have been able to live... You saved her. She'll never forget that!'

'And where is your little girl now?' asked the doctor; he was very excited.

Then the old clown went up to one of the canvas partitions and called. He said a strange name, pronouncing two sounds as though he had opened up a small, round, wooden box which is difficult to open:

'Suok!'

Several seconds passed. Then a canvas flap was raised a little, and out peered a little girl with her head slightly bent and with tousled curls. She looked at the doctor with grey eyes, a little from below, attentively and mischievously.

The doctor raised his eyes and was stupefied: it was Tutti the Heir's doll!

Part Three

Suok

A Difficult Role for a Young Actress

Yes, it was her!

But where had she sprung from, the devil take it? Miracles? What miracles! Dr Gaspar knew very well that there are no miracles. This, he decided, was simply a trick. It was a living doll, and, when he had been incautious enough to fall asleep in the carriage, it had slipped away, like a disobedient little girl.

'There's nothing to smile about! Your ingratiating smile doesn't make you any less blameworthy,' he said sternly. 'As you can see, fate has punished you. Completely by chance I've found you where it didn't seem possible to do so.'

The doll goggled. Then it began blinking like a little rabbit, and threw a perplexed look in the direction of Augustus the clown. The latter sighed.

'Who are you, give me a straight answer!' The doctor put all the severity he could into his voice. But the doll looked so charming that it was hard to be angry.

'You see,' she said, 'you've forgotten me. I'm Suok.'

'Su-ok,' repeated the doctor. 'But you're Tutti the Heir's doll, aren't you?'

'What do you mean, doll! I'm an ordinary little girl...'

'What?... You're pretending!'

The doll came out from behind the partition. The lamp cast a bright light upon her. She was smiling, with her tousled head tilted to one side. Her hair was the same colour as the feathers of little grey birds.

The furry animal in the cage watched her very attentively.

Dr Gaspar was utterly bewildered. In a little while the reader will learn the whole secret. But now we want to give the reader notice of one very important fact which had eluded the attentive gaze of Dr Gaspar Arneri. At moments of excitement a man sometimes fails to notice facts which, as adults say, are staring him in the face.

And this is that fact: now, in the wagon, the doll looked completely different.

Her grey eyes were shining merrily. She seemed serious and attentive now, but not a trace remained of her sadness. On the contrary, you would have said that this was a mischievous girl pretending to be a demure one.

And then the next thing. Where on earth had her former magnificent dress got to, all that pink silk, the gold roses, the lace, the sequins, the fairytale costume thanks to which any little girl might have looked, if not like a princess, then in any event like a Christmas-tree decoration? Now, just imagine, the doll was dressed more than modestly. A smock with a blue sailor's collar, and old shoes that were grey enough not to be white. She had nothing on inside the shoes. Don't think that because of this simple costume the doll had become ugly. On the contrary, it suited her. You do come across grubby children like that: at first you don't favour them with a glance, but then, after looking more carefully, you see that this grubby child is prettier than a princess, particularly as princesses sometimes turn into frogs, or frogs, on the contrary, turn into princesses.

But this is the main thing: you remember there were terrible black wounds on the chest of Tutti the Heir's doll. And now they had disappeared.

This was a cheerful, healthy doll!

But Dr Gaspar had noticed nothing. Perhaps he would have worked out what was going on at the very next moment, but at precisely that next moment somebody knocked on the door. At this point things became even more confused. Into the wagon came the black man.

The doll began squealing, and the animal in the cage spat, although it wasn't a cat, but some more complicated creature.

We already know who the black man was. Dr Gaspar, who had made this black man out of the most ordinary Tibullus, knew it too. But nobody else knew the secret.

The confusion continued for five minutes. The black man behaved in the most appalling manner. He grabbed the doll, lifted it up in the air and began kissing it on the cheeks and the nose, at which the nose and the cheeks were turned away so energetically that, as he kissed them, the black man might have been compared with someone trying to bite an apple that's hanging on a string.

Old Augustus had shut his eyes and, terror-stricken, was rocking about like a Chinese emperor trying to decide whether to cut off a criminal's head or to make him eat a live rat without sugar.

The shoe flew off one of the doll's feet and hit the lamp. The lamp overturned and gave up the ghost. It became dark. The horror was at its height. Then everyone saw that dawn had begun to break. The cracks around the door were lit up.

'It's already dawn,' said Dr Gaspar, 'and I need to go to the Palace of the Three Fat Men with Tutti the Heir's doll.'

The black man gave the door a push. Grey light from the street entered the dwelling. The clown was sitting as before, and his eyes were shut. The doll had hidden behind the partition.

Dr Gaspar hurriedly explained to Tibullus how things stood. He told him the whole story of Tutti the Heir's doll, of how it had disappeared, and how it had fortunately now been found here in the wagon.

The doll was listening closely behind the partition and didn't understand a thing.

'He's calling him Tibullus,' she thought in surprise. 'How on earth can he be Tibullus? He's an awful black man. Tibullus is handsome, and he's white, not black…'

Then she stuck one eye out and had a look. From the pocket of his red trousers the black man took an elongated flask, he opened it, which made the flask let out a squeak like a sparrow, and began pouring some sort of liquid over himself from the flask. A second later a miracle took place: the black man became white, handsome, and not black. No doubt remained. It was Tibullus!

'Hurrah!' the doll cried, and flew out from behind the partition straight onto Tibullus' neck.

The clown, who had seen nothing and had decided that the most awful thing had happened, fell off what he had been sitting on and remained motionless. Tibullus picked him up by the trousers.

Now it was the turn of the doll, without any invitation, to smother Tibullus with kisses.

'What a marvellous thing!' she said, breathless in her delight. 'How is it you were so black? I didn't recognise you.'

'Suok!' Tibullus said sternly.

She immediately jumped down from his enormous chest and stood to attention in front of him no worse than a good little tin soldier.

'What?' she asked like a schoolgirl.

Tibullus laid his hands on her tousled head. She looked at him from below with happy grey eyes.

'Did you hear what Dr Gaspar was saying?'

'Yes. He was saying that the Three Fat Men had charged him with healing Tutti the Heir's doll. He said that the doll had slipped out of his carriage. He says that I'm the doll.'

'He's wrong,' Tibullus declared. 'Dr Gaspar, this isn't a doll, I can assure you. This is my little friend, this is a little girl, Suok the dancer, my faithful comrade in circus work.'

'It's true!' said the delighted doll. 'After all, you and I have walked the wire together any number of times.'

She was very pleased that Tibullus had called her his faithful comrade.

'Dear Tibullus!' she whispered, and rubbed her face on his hand.

'What?' the doctor questioned. 'Is it really a living girl? Suok, you say?... Yes! Yes! Indeed! I can see it clearly now. I'm remembering. I saw this little girl once, didn't I. Yes... Yes... I saved her, didn't I, from an old woman's servants who wanted to beat her with sticks!'

Here the doctor even clasped his hands together.

'Ha-ha-ha! Why yes, of course. And that was why the little face of Tutti the Heir's doll seemed so familiar to me. It's a simply amazing resemblance, or, as they say in science, a phenomenon.'

All had been cleared up to the delight of everyone.

It was getting lighter and lighter. In a backyard a cockerel gave a groan.

And here the doctor became sad again.

'Yes, this is all splendid. But it means that I don't have Tutti the Heir's doll, it means that I really have lost it...'

'It means that you've found it,' said Tibullus, hugging the little girl tight.

'What do you mean?'

'What I said. Do you understand me, Suok?'

'I think so,' Suok answered quietly.

'Well?' asked Tibullus.

'Of course,' the doll said, and smiled.

The doctor hadn't understood a thing.

'Did you do as I said when you and I used to perform in front of a crowd on Sundays? You stood on the striped platform. I said, "*Allez*", and you stepped down onto the wire and walked towards me. I waited for you in the middle, very high above the crowd. I put one knee forward, again said to you

"*Allez!*" – and you got up onto my knee, then climbed up onto my shoulders... Were you frightened?'

'No. You said "*Allez!*", so I had to be calm and not be afraid of anything.'

'Well, then,' said Tibullus, 'I'm saying "*Allez!*" to you now as well. You'll be the doll.'

'I'll be the doll.'

'She'll be the doll?' Dr Gaspar queried. 'What does that mean?'

I hope that you, reader, have understood! You haven't had to endure so much excitement and surprise as Dr Gaspar, and so you're calmer and can grasp things more quickly.

Just think: the doctor hadn't yet had a proper sleep, after all. As it is, you really have to wonder at his iron constitution.

There hadn't been time for a second cockerel to wake up before everything was decided. Tibullus developed a detailed plan of action:

'Suok, you're an artiste. I think, in spite of your age, you're not a bad artiste at all. When the pantomime *The Foolish King* was on in our show in the spring, you played the part of the Golden Cabbage-stalk splendidly. Then in the ballet you had the role of a transfer, and gave a wonderful representation of the miller's transformation into a teapot. You dance better than anyone and sing better than anyone, you have a good imagination and – the most important thing – you're a brave and quick-witted little girl.'

Suok stood, red with happiness. She even felt awkward at all this praise.

'And so you must take the role of Tutti the Heir's doll.'

Suok clapped her hands and kissed everyone in turn: Tibullus, old Augustus and Dr Gaspar.

'Wait,' Tibullus continued, 'that's not all. You know Prospero the armourer is in an iron cage in the Palace of the Three Fat Men. You must free Prospero the armourer.'

'Open the cage?'

'Yes. I know a secret that will give Prospero the chance to escape from the palace.'

'A secret?'

'Yes. There's an underground passage there.'

Here Tibullus told them about the children's balloon seller.

'The start of the passage is in a saucepan somewhere – probably in the palace kitchen. You're going to find the passage.'

'Very well.'

The sun hadn't yet risen, but the birds were already awake. The plot of grass that could be seen from the doors of the wagon had turned green.

In the light, the mysterious animal in the cage turned out to be an ordinary fox.

'We can't waste time! There's a long road before us.'

Dr Gaspar said,

'Now you must choose the prettiest of your dresses…'

Suok brought all of her costumes. They were delightful, because Suok herself had made them. Like any talented actress, she was blessed with good taste.

Dr Gaspar spent a long time rummaging in the multi-coloured pile.

'Why,' he said, 'I think this dress will be perfectly suitable. It's not a bit inferior to the one that was on the maimed doll. Put it on!'

Suok got changed. In the twinkling of the rising sun she stood in the middle of the wagon looking so smart that it's unlikely any birthday-girl in the world could have competed with her. The dress was pink. And at moments when Suok made a certain sort of movement, it seemed as if golden rain were falling. The dress twinkled, rustled and smelled sweet.

'I'm ready,' said Suok.

The farewells lasted a minute. People who perform in the circus don't like tears. They risk their lives too often. Besides, they couldn't embrace one another too warmly in case they spoilt the dress.

'Come back soon!' said old Augustus, and heaved a sigh.

'I'm going to the workers' districts. We have to make a count of our forces. The workers are expecting me. They've learnt that I'm alive and at liberty.'

Tibullus wrapped himself in his cape, put on a wide-brimmed hat, dark glasses, and the big false nose which formed part of the pasha's costume in the pantomime *The March to Cairo*.

In this guise, he couldn't be recognised. True, the huge nose did make him ugly, but on the other hand unrecognisable.

Old Augustus stood on the threshold. The doctor, Tibullus and Suok left the wagon.

The day had come into its own.

'Quickly! Quickly!' the doctor hurried them.

A minute later he was already sitting in the carriage along with Suok.

'You're not afraid?' he asked.

Suok smiled in reply. The doctor kissed her on the forehead.

The streets were still deserted. Human voices were heard rarely. But suddenly the loud barking of a dog rang out. Then the dog yelped and growled, as though someone was taking a bone away from it.

The doctor looked out of the carriage.

Imagine, it was the same dog that had bitten Lapitup the strongman! But that wasn't all.

The doctor saw the following. The dog was struggling with a man. A tall, slim man with a small head, who looked like a grasshopper and wore a beautiful but strange costume, was trying to tear something pink, beautiful and unidentifiable away from the dog. Pink shreds were flying in all directions.

The man was victorious. He snatched away his spoils and, pressing them to his chest, he started running in precisely the direction from which the doctor was driving.

And when he met the carriage, Suok, who was looking from behind the doctor's back, saw something terrible. The strange man wasn't running, but speeding along in elegant leaps, scarcely touching the ground, like a ballet dancer. The green flaps of his tailcoat flew behind him like the sails of a windmill. And in his arms – in his arms he held a little girl with black wounds on her chest.

'It's me!' cried Suok.

She recoiled into the depths of the carriage and hid her face in the plush cushion.

Hearing the cry, the abductor looked round, and then Dr Gaspar recognised in him Onetwothreesir the dancing-master.

A Doll with a Good Appetite

Tutti the Heir was standing on the terrace. The geography teacher was looking through a pair of binoculars. Tutti the Heir was demanding that a compass be brought. But that was unnecessary.

Tutti the Heir was awaiting the arrival of the doll.

His great excitement had made him sleep soundly and sweetly all through the night.

Visible from the terrace was the road from the town gates to the palace. The sun, which was coming out over the town, was making it difficult to look. The Heir was holding the palms of his hands next to his eyes, pulling a wry face and feeling sorry that he couldn't sneeze.

'There's still no one to be seen,' said the geography teacher.

He had been entrusted with this responsible work because, through his speciality, he was best of all able to understand distances, horizons, moving points and other such things.

'But maybe there is?' insisted Tutti.

'Don't argue with me. Besides the binoculars, I have knowledge and an accurate conception of objects. Now I can see some jasmine bushes, which have a Latin name that is very beautiful but hard to remember. Further on I can see bridges and guardsmen with butterflies flying around them, and then there's the road… I beg your pardon! I beg your pardon!'

He twisted the binoculars. Tutti the Heir stood on tiptoe. His heart began pounding from the bottom up, as though he hadn't done his homework.

'Yes,' said the teacher.

And at that moment three horsemen set off towards the road from the direction of the palace park. It was Captain Bonaventura and the watch galloping to meet the carriage which had appeared on the road.

'Hurrah!' cried the Heir, so shrilly that geese in distant villages responded.

Down below the terrace the gymnastics instructor stood in readiness to catch the Heir in flight, should his delight cause him to topple over the terrace's stone wall.

And so, Dr Gaspar's carriage was bowling along towards the palace. Binoculars and the scholarly knowledge of the geography teacher were no longer needed. Everyone could already see the carriage and the white horse.

A happy moment! The carriage stopped by the last bridge. The guardsmen on watch made way. The Heir waved both his arms and jumped up and down, shaking his golden hair. And finally he saw the most important thing: a little man climbed out of the carriage, awkwardly, his age evident from his movements. The guardsmen, holding their sabres deferentially and saluting, stood at a short distance. The little man took out from the carriage a wonderful doll, like a fresh pink bouquet interwoven with ribbons.

It was an enchanting picture beneath the deepening blue of the morning sky, in the radiance of the grass and the sun.

A minute later the doll was already in the palace. The meeting took place in the following way.

The doll walked unassisted.

Oh, Suok played her role splendidly! Had she fallen into the company of the most genuine dolls, they would without any doubt have taken her for a doll just like themselves.

She was calm. She sensed she was a success in the role.

'There are things that are harder,' she thought, 'juggling, for example, with a lighted lamp, or doing a double somersault...'

And Suok had had occasion to do both the one and the other in the circus.

In a word, Suok was unafraid. She was even enjoying this game. Much more agitated was Dr Gaspar. He walked behind Suok. She took tiny little steps, like a ballerina walking on her points. Her dress stirred, trembled and rustled.

The parquet floors gleamed. She was reflected in them as a pink cloud. She was very small in the midst of the lofty halls, which were increased in depth by the brilliance of the parquet, and in width by mirrors.

She might have been thought to be a little basket of flowers floating across a huge expanse of still water.

She walked, cheerful and smiling, past the guards, past the leather and iron men who watched as if spellbound, and past officials who smiled for the first time in their lives.

They stepped aside before her, letting her pass, as though she were the mistress of this palace coming into her own.

It became so quiet that her light steps could be heard, sounding no louder than the falling of petals.

And from above, down the widest of staircases, Tutti the Heir, just as small and radiant, came to meet the doll.

They were the same height.

Suok stopped.

'So here he is, Tutti the Heir,' she thought.

Before her stood a slim boy who looked like an angry little girl, grey-eyed and a little sad, with his tousled head bent to one side.

Suok knew who Tutti was. Suok knew who the Three Fat Men were. She knew that the Three Fat Men had taken all the iron, all the coal, all the grain procured by the hands of the poor, hungry people. She remembered very well the grand old woman who had set her lackeys on little Suok. She knew they were all the same crowd: the Three Fat Men, the grand old women, the dandies, the shopkeepers, the guardsmen – all those who had put Prospero the armourer in an iron cage and had been hunting her friend, Tibullus the acrobat.

While she had been walking into the palace, she had thought that Tutti the Heir would seem repulsive to her, something like the grand old woman, only with a long, thin, crimson tongue always sticking out.

But she didn't feel any repulsion. She rather began to feel glad at having seen him.

She looked at him with merry grey eyes.

'Is it you, doll?' asked Tutti the Heir, reaching out his hand.

'What on earth am I to do?' thought Suok in fright. 'Can dolls talk? Oh dear, I wasn't told!… I don't know how the doll the guardsmen killed used to behave…'

But Dr Gaspar came to her aid.

'Master Heir,' he began solemnly, 'I have cured your doll. As you can see, not only did I return life to her, I also made that life more remarkable. The doll has, without doubt, become prettier, then she's got a magnificent new dress, and, most important of all – I've taught your doll to talk, to write songs and to dance.'

'What joy!' the Heir said quietly.

'It's time to act,' thought Suok.

And at this point the little actress from Uncle Brizak's travelling show made her debut on a new stage.

That stage was the main ballroom of the palace. And masses of spectators had gathered. They crowded around on all sides: at the tops of the staircases, in the passageways, in the gallery. They climbed in through the round windows, filled the balconies to overflowing and clambered up onto columns, the better to see and hear.

A multitude of heads and backs of the most varied colours and hues burned in the bright sunlight.

Suok saw a multitude of faces looking at her and smiling broadly.

The cooks with their open palms and fingers, from which, like sap from branches, flowed sweet red juices or rich brown sauces; the ministers in multi-coloured, embroidered uniforms, like monkeys dressed up as cockerels; plump little musicians in tight tailcoats; ladies and gentlemen of the court, hunch-backed doctors, long-nosed scholars, shock-headed heralds; retainers dressed up no worse than ministers.

This entire mass was clinging to everything that could be clung to.

And everyone was silent. With bated breath, everyone was watching the little pink creature, who calmly, and with the great dignity of a twelve-year-old girl, met the hundred gazes. She wasn't at all embarrassed. This audience was unlikely to be more demanding than the audiences in the squares where Suok performed almost every day. Oh, those audiences were really demanding: loafers, soldiers, actors, schoolchildren, small tradesmen! Suok wasn't afraid even of them. And they would say,

'Suok is the best actress in the world!…'

And they would throw their last small change onto her rug. When at the same time, for that small coin, a liver pie could be bought, which would serve as some hosier's breakfast, dinner and supper.

And now Suok really began playing her part as a doll.

She brought the toes of her shoes together, then she rose up onto them, she lifted her arms, bent at the elbows, up to her face, and, moving both of her little fingers in the manner of a Chinese mandarin, she started singing a song. As she did so, she rocked her head to the left and the right in time with the tune.

She smiled coquettishly and mischievously. But all the time she tried to make her eyes round and wide, as all dolls' eyes are.

This is what she sang:

Over crucibles' bright burning
Dr Gaspar toiled, and then,
With his famous skill and learning,
Brought me back to life again.
Take a look: you see me smiling.
Listen as I heave a sigh…
Yes, I'm happy and beguiling,
And I didn't have to die.
All my life to you I'm steering,
Though they try my path to block!…
Don't forget that name endearing
Of your sister sweet – Suok!
I can't bear to be without you,
And, while dropping off to sleep,
I just had a dream about you –
And I saw the way you weep!
Look: my lashes have a tear in,
On my brow's an errant lock,

Don't forget that name endearing
Of your sister sweet – Suok!

'Suok,' Tutti repeated quietly.

His eyes were full of tears, which made it look as if he had not two eyes, but four.

The doll finished the song and dropped a curtsey. The ballroom heaved a sigh of admiration. Everyone began moving, nodding their heads and clicking their tongues.

The melody of the song was, indeed, charming, albeit somewhat sad for such a young voice, and the voice itself sounded so delightful, it was as if it had been coming from a throat of silver or glass.

'She sings like an angel,' the words of the conductor rang out in the silence.

'Only her song is a little strange,' remarked some dignitary or other, while his medal clinked.

With this, all criticism stopped short. Into the ballroom came the Three Fat Men. They might have found the crowd of onlookers unpleasant, and everyone rushed for the exits. In the turmoil, a cook stuck his open hand with its entire supply of raspberry juice right on some beauty's back. The beauty screamed, whereupon it came to light that she had false teeth, because the teeth fell out. A fat guards captain stepped on the attractive teeth with his unattractive, common boot.

There came the sounds: crunch, crunch! – and the Master of Ceremonies, who happened to be there too, let out a curse:

'Who's been throwing nuts around? They're cracking underfoot! It's a disgrace!'

The beauty who had lost her false teeth wanted to cry out, and even threw her arms up in the air, but – alas! – her voice had perished along with her teeth. She could only mumble something barely intelligible.

After a minute, no one superfluous was left in the ballroom. Only people of responsibility remained.

And now Suok and Dr Gaspar stood before the Three Fat Men.

The Three Fat Men didn't seem perturbed by the events of the day before. They had just been playing ball in the park under the supervision of the duty doctor. This was done for the sake of the exercise. They were very tired. Their sweaty faces were shining. Their shirts were stuck to their backs, and those backs looked like sails, puffed out by the wind. Beneath his eye, one of them had a dark bruise in the shape of an unattractive rose or of an attractive frog. One of the other Fat Men threw fearful glances at this unattractive rose.

'That one threw the ball in his face and gave him a beautiful bruise,' thought Suok.

The injured Fat Man's breathing was heavy and menacing. Dr Gaspar smiled in confusion. The Fat Men examined the doll in silence. The radiant look of Tutti the Heir put them in a good mood.

'Well then,' said one, 'so you're Dr Gaspar Arneri?'

The doctor bowed.

'Well, how's the doll?' asked another.

'It's wonderful!' exclaimed Tutti.

The Fat Men had never seen him so animated.

'That's excellent! It really does look good...'

The First Fat Man wiped his forehead with the palm of his hand, wheezed bad-temperedly and said:

'Dr Gaspar, you've carried out our command. You now have the right to demand a reward.'

Silence fell.

A little secretary in a ginger wig held his quill at the ready to make a note of the doctor's demand.

The doctor began spelling out his request:

'Ten scaffolds were built in Court Square yesterday for the execution of the men who rose…'

'They'll be executed today,' one of the Fat Men interrupted.

'And that's precisely what I'm getting at. My request is this: I ask that you grant all the prisoners their lives and their freedom. I ask that you cancel the execution entirely and burn those scaffolds down…'

On hearing this request, the ginger secretary dropped his quill in horror. The quill, which had been very well sharpened, went into the Second Fat Man's foot. He cried out and began spinning on one leg. The First Fat Man, the owner of the bruise, chuckled at his misfortune: he was avenged.

'What the devil!' yelled the Second Fat Man, trying to pull the quill out of his foot like an arrow. 'What the devil! That request is criminal! How dare you demand such things!'

The ginger secretary ran for it. A vase of flowers that he overturned on his way flew after him and exploded into pieces like a bomb. There was complete uproar. The Fat Man pulled the quill out and flung it in the wake of the secretary. But how can you possibly be a good javelin-thrower when you're so fat! The quill hit one of the guardsmen on sentry duty in the backside. But, being a zealous veteran, he remained motionless. The quill continued to stick out of an inappropriate spot until the changing of the guard.

'I demand that all the workers condemned to death be granted their lives. I demand that the scaffolds be burned down,' the doctor repeated, not loudly, but firmly.

The cries of the Fat Men rang out in response. The resultant impression was of someone cracking bits of wood.

'No! No! No! Certainly not! They will be executed!'

'Die,' the doctor whispered to the doll.

Suok realised what he meant. Again she rose onto the points of her toes, let out a squeak and tottered. Her dress began to flutter like the wings of a captured butterfly and her head drooped – the doll was ready to fall at any second.

The Heir threw himself towards her.

'Oh! Oh!' he cried.

Suok let out an even sadder squeak.

'There,' said Dr Gaspar, 'you see? The doll will lose its life again. The mechanism inside it is too sensitive. The doll will be damaged for good unless you carry out my request. I don't think the Heir will be very pleased if his doll becomes a useless pink rag.'

The Heir was gripped by rage. He began stamping his feet like a baby elephant. He screwed his eyes up tight and began shaking his head.

'Not for anything! Not for anything, you hear!' he cried. 'Carry out the doctor's request! I won't give up my doll! Suok! Suok!' he sobbed.

Of course, the Fat Men gave in. The order was given. The pardon was announced. A happy Dr Gaspar set off for home.

'I shall sleep for a whole day,' he mused on the way.

As he rode into town he could already hear conversations about the scaffolds burning in Court Square, and the rich being very unhappy that the executions of the poor wouldn't be taking place.

And so Suok remained in the Palace of the Three Fat Men.

Tutti went out into the garden with her.

The Heir trampled on some flowers, cut himself on some barbed wire and almost fell into a pool. In his happiness, he didn't notice a thing.

'Does he really not understand that I'm a living girl?' wondered Suok. 'I wouldn't let myself be fooled like this.'

Breakfast was brought. Suok saw some pieces of cake and remembered that only in the autumn of the previous year had she had the good fortune to eat just one cake. And even then, old Augustus had claimed that it wasn't a cake but ginger-bread. Tutti the Heir's cakes were magnificent. Ten bees congregated around them, taking them for flowers.

'What am I to do?' Suok agonised. 'Dolls don't eat, do they? But there are different sorts of doll... Oh, how I want a cake!'

And Suok couldn't contain herself.

'I want a little piece...' she said quietly. A flush covered her cheeks.

'That's good!' said the Heir in delight. 'You didn't want to eat before. I was so bored before, eating breakfast by myself. Oh, what a good thing! You've got an appetite now.'

And Suok ate a little piece of cake. Then another one, and another, and another. And suddenly she saw that a servant, who was watching over the Heir from a distance, was looking at her, and he was looking at her, what's more, in horror.

The servant's mouth was wide open.

The servant was right.

He had never had occasion to see dolls eating.

Suok took fright and dropped her fourth piece of cake, the very crumbliest and with a grape on the top.

But it turned out all right. The servant rubbed his eyes and closed his mouth.

'I just imagined it. It's the heat!'

The Heir talked incessantly. Then, getting tired, he fell silent.

It was very quiet at that hot hour. The previous day's wind had evidently flown a long way away. Now everything was still. Even the birds weren't flying about.

And in the silence, Suok, who was sitting on the grass next to the Heir, heard a strange, regularly repeated sound, like the ticking of a clock hidden in cotton wool. Only a clock goes 'tick-tock', while the sound now was like this: 'knock-knock'.

'What's that?' she asked.

'What?' The Heir raised his eyebrows, like an adult in a moment of surprise.

'There: knock-knock... Is it a clock? Have you got a watch?'

Silence set in again, and again in the silence there was something knocking. Suok raised a finger. The Heir listened carefully.

'It's not a clock,' he said quietly. 'It's the beating of my iron heart...'

The Menagerie

At two o'clock, Tutti the Heir was called into the classroom. It was time for lessons. Suok remained alone.

No one, of course, suspected that Suok was a living girl. In all probability, Tutti the Heir's real doll, which was now in the hands of Onetwothreesir the dancing-master, had behaved no less naturally. It must have been a very skilled craftsman who had made that doll. True, it hadn't eaten pastries. But perhaps Tutti the Heir was right. Perhaps it really had simply had no appetite.

And so Suok remained alone.

Her situation was a difficult one.

An enormous palace, a tangle of entrances, galleries, staircases.

Terrifying guardsmen, unknown stern people in differently coloured wigs, quietness and splendour.

No one paid her any attention.

She stood in the Heir's bedroom, by the window.

'I must work out a plan of action,' she decided. 'The iron cage with Prospero the armourer is in Tutti the Heir's menagerie. I need to get inside the menagerie.' You already know that the Heir wasn't shown any real children. He was never taken to town, not even in a closed carriage. He had grown up in the palace. He was taught various branches of learning, he was read books about cruel tsars and military commanders. The people who surrounded him were forbidden to smile. All of his tutors and teachers were tall, thin old men with tightly pursed lips and cheekbones the colour of gunpowder. What's more, they all suffered from indigestion. And a man with that condition doesn't feel like smiling.

Tutti the Heir had never heard merry, ringing laughter. Only at times did the guffaws of some drunken sausage-maker reach him, or those of the Fat Men themselves, entertaining their no-less-fat guests. But could that really be called laughter? It was an awful bellowing, which made you feel not merry, but afraid.

Only the doll had smiled. But the doll's smile hadn't seemed dangerous to the Fat Men. And besides, the doll had been silent. She couldn't have told Tutti the Heir about the many things hidden from him by the palace park and by the guards with their drums at the iron bridges. And so he knew nothing about the people, about poverty, about hungry children, about factories, mines and prisons, about the peasants, about how the rich forced the poor to labour and took everything that was made by the thin hands of the poor for themselves.

The Three Fat Men wanted to bring up a fierce, cruel Heir. He was deprived of the company of children and had a menagerie set up for him.

'Let him look at wild animals,' they decided. 'He's already got a dead, soulless doll, and now he'll have some fierce wild animals. Let him see how tigers are fed raw meat, and how a boa constrictor swallows a live rabbit. Let him hear the voices of predatory wild animals and look into their red, devilish pupils. Then he'll learn to be cruel.'

But things didn't turn out as the Fat Men wanted.

Tutti the Heir studied diligently, listened to terrible chronicles of heroes and tsars, and looked with hatred at the spotty noses of tutors, but he didn't become cruel.

He came to love the company of the doll more than the company of the wild animals.

Of course, you can say it's a disgrace for a twelve-year-old boy to be amusing himself with dolls. At that age many would prefer to be hunting tigers. But there was a certain reason for it, which will be revealed in good time.

Let us return to Suok.

She had decided to wait until the evening. Indeed, a doll roaming through the palace by itself in broad daylight might arouse suspicion.

They met again after lessons.

'You know,' said Suok, 'when I was lying sick at Dr Gaspar's, I had a nightmare. I dreamt that I'd turned from a doll into a living girl… And it was as if I were a circus artiste. I lived in a travelling show with other artistes. The show moved about from place to place, stopping at fairs and in big squares, and it organised performances. I walked the tightrope, I danced, knew how to do difficult acrobatic tricks, played different roles in pantomimes…'

The Heir listened to her with eyes open wide.

'We were very poor. Very often we didn't eat… We had a big white horse. It was called Anra. I rode it and juggled, standing on a broad saddle covered with torn yellow satin. And the horse died, because for a whole month we had too little money to feed it properly…'

'Poor?' asked Tutti. 'I don't understand. Why were you poor?'

'We performed in front of poor people. Poor people would throw us small copper coins. But sometimes after a performance, the hat with which Augustus the clown went among the spectators remained completely empty.'

Tutti the Heir didn't understand a thing.

And Suok talked to him until the evening came. She talked about the harsh life of the beggarly, about the big town, about the grand old woman who had wanted her thrashed, about the live children that the rich set their dogs on, about Tibullus the acrobat and Prospero the armourer, about how the workers, miners and sailors wanted to destroy the authority of the rich and the fat.

Most of all she talked about the circus. She gradually got carried away and forgot she was recounting a dream.

'I've been living in Uncle Brizak's travelling show for a very long time. I can't even remember since when I've known how to dance, and ride a horse, and swing on the trapeze. Oh, the wonderful tricks I've learnt!' she clasped her hands together. 'Last Sunday, for example, we were performing at the harbour. I was playing a waltz on apricot stones...'

'What do you mean, on apricot stones?'

'Oh, you don't know? Haven't you ever seen a whistle made from an apricot stone? It's very simple. I collected twelve stones and made whistles out of them. Well, I rubbed and rubbed them on a rock until there was a little hole...'

'How interesting!'

'It's not just on twelve stones that you can whistle a waltz. I know how to whistle with a key as well...'

'A key? How? Show me. I've got a marvellous key...'

With these words, Tutti the Heir unbuttoned the collar of his jacket and took from his neck a fine chain on which there dangled a small white key.

'There!'

'Why do you hide it on your chest?' asked Suok.

'The Chancellor gave me this key. It's the key to one of the cages in my menagerie.'

'And do you keep the keys to all the cages hidden about you?'

'No. But I was told this is the most important key. I have to look after it…'

Suok demonstrated her art to the Heir. She whistled a marvellous song, holding the key with the little hole uppermost beside her pursed lips.

The Heir went into such raptures that he even forgot about the key he had been instructed to look after. The key remained with Suok. She put it mechanically into her pink, lacy pocket.

Evening came.

A special room had been prepared for the doll next to Tutti the Heir's bedroom.

Tutti the Heir slept and dreamt of amazing things: funny, big-nosed masks; a man carrying a huge, smoothly dressed stone on his bare yellow back, and a fat man striking this other one with a black lash; a ragged little boy who was eating a potato, and a grand old woman in lace who was riding a white horse and whistling some repellent waltz with the help of twelve apricot stones.

And at the same time, in a completely different spot, at one end of the palace park and a long way from that little bedroom, the following was taking place. Don't worry, though, it wasn't anything in particular. But Tutti the Heir wasn't the only one having amazing dreams that night. The guardsman who'd fallen asleep on duty at the entrance to Tutti the Heir's menagerie had a dream that merited surprise as well.

He was sitting on a stone pillar, leaning his back against a railing, and dozing sweetly. His sabre lay between his knees in its wide, shining scabbard. A pistol was poking out very peacefully from the black silk scarf at his side. On the gravel next to him stood a latticed lantern, which lit up the guardsman's boots and a long caterpillar which had fallen from some leaves directly onto his sleeve.

The scene seemed completely peaceful.

And so, the sentry slept and had an extraordinary dream. He dreamt that Tutti the Heir's doll came up to him. It was exactly the same as in the morning, when Dr Gaspar Arneri had brought it: the same pink dress, bows, lace, sequins. Only now, in the dream, the doll turned out to be a living girl. She moved freely, but she was stealthy and jumpy, looking around to one side and then the other, and she kept on putting a finger to her lips.

The lantern lit up the whole of her little figure.

The guardsman even smiled as he slept.

Then he sighed and settled himself more comfortably, leaning a shoulder against the railing and sticking his nose into an iron rose in the railing's pattern.

And then, seeing that the sentry was asleep, Suok picked up the lantern and tiptoed cautiously inside the fence.

The guardsman was snoring, but to him, as he slept, it seemed to be the tigers in the menagerie roaring.

In fact, the menagerie was quiet. The animals were asleep.

The lantern lit up only a small area. Suok moved slowly, peering into the darkness. Fortunately, the night wasn't dark. It was lit up by the stars and by the light of the lanterns hanging in the park, which reached this remote spot through the tops of the trees and buildings.

From the fence, the girl went down a short path between low-growing shrubs, covered with white flowers of some sort.

Then all at once she smelt the animals. The smell was familiar to her: a tamer had once travelled with the show with his three lions and a Great Dane.

Suok emerged into a small open square. It was black all around, as though there were little houses standing there.

'Cages,' whispered Suok.

Her heart was beating hard.

She wasn't afraid of wild animals, because people who perform in the circus aren't in general cowardly. She was only worried that one of the animals might be woken by her footsteps and the light of the lantern, might start growling and rouse the sentry.

She approached the cages.

'Where ever is Prospero?' she worried.

She lifted the lantern higher and looked into the cages. All was motionless and quiet. The light of the lantern broke on the bars of the cages and flew down in uneven pieces onto the bodies of the creatures sleeping behind those bars.

She saw thick, hairy ears, sometimes an outstretched paw, sometimes a striped back. The eagles slept with their wings open, and looked like ancient coats of arms. In the depths of some cages was the blackness of some unrecognisable huge shapes.

In one cage, behind slender silvery bars, on perches at different heights, sat some parrots. And when Suok stopped by this cage, it seemed to her as if the one sitting closest of all to the bars, an old parrot with a long, red beard, opened one eye and looked at her. And its eye was like a blind lemon pip.

And what's more, it quickly closed the eye, as though pretending to be asleep. At the same time it seemed to Suok that it smiled into its red beard.

'I'm simply an idiot,' Suok reassured herself. Nonetheless, she had begun to feel afraid.

Time and again, now here, now there, something would click, crunch or squeak in the quietness.

Try going into a stable in the night, or listen closely to a henhouse: you'll be struck by the quietness, and at the same time you'll hear a great number of little sounds – now the movement of a wing, now a champing noise, now the cracking of a roost, now a thin voice, slipping out like a little drop of liquid from the throat of a sleeping bird.

'Where ever is Prospero?' thought Suok once again, but already with greater alarm. 'What if they executed him today and put an eagle in his cage?'

And at that point, from out of the darkness, someone's hoarse voice said:

'Suok!'

And at once she heard heavy, rapid breathing and some other sounds too, as though a large, sick dog were whimpering.

'Oh!' cried Suok.

She swung the lantern in the direction from which she had been called. There were two little reddish lights burning there. A large black creature like a bear was standing in a cage, holding on to the bars and pressing its head against them.

'Prospero!' Suok said quietly.

And in one second she had thought through a whole heap of ideas.

'Why does he look so awful? He's covered in hair, like a bear. He's got red sparks in his eyes. He's got long, curved claws. He's got no clothes on. He's not a man, but a gorilla.'

Suok was ready to burst into tears.

'You've come at last, Suok,' said the strange creature. 'I knew I'd see you.'

'Hello. I've come to set you free,' said Suok in a quavering voice.

'I shan't leave this cage. I'm going to die today.'

And the terrible whimpering noises were heard again. The creature fell down, then picked itself up and pressed itself against the bars once more.

'Come closer, Suok.'

Suok went closer. A frightening face was looking at her. It wasn't a human face, of course. More than anything it looked like the face of a wolf. And most frightening of all was the fact that the ears of this wolf were the shape of human ears, even though they were covered in a short, rough coat of hair.

Suok wanted to cover her eyes with the palm of her hand. In the other hand the lantern was jumping. Yellow patches of light were flying through the air.

'You're afraid of me, Suok... I've lost the look of a human being. Don't be afraid! Come closer... You've grown, got thinner. You have a sad little face...'

He spoke with difficulty. He was slipping ever lower, and he finally lay down on the wooden floor of his cage. His breathing was more and more rapid, and he was opening wide a mouth full of long, yellow teeth.

'I'm going to die now. I knew I'd see you before I died.'

He reached out his shaggy, apelike arm. He was searching for something in the darkness. There was a sound as of a nail being pulled out of something, and then the terrible arm reached out through the bars.

In its hand was a little board.

'Take this. Everything's written down here.'

Suok hid the board away.

'Prospero,' she said quietly.

There was no reply.

Suok brought the lantern closer. The teeth were bared for ever. The dull, stilled eyes looked right through her.

'Prospero!' cried Suok, dropping the lantern. 'He's dead! He's dead! Prospero!'

The lantern went out.

Part Four

Prospero the Armourer

The Destruction of the Confectionary

The guardsman we met at the entrance to the menagerie at the very moment when Suok pinched the latticed lantern from him was woken by the noise that had started up in the menagerie.

The animals were growling, howling, squeaking; wings were clapping; tails were striking against iron bars.

The guardsman yawned with a terrible cracking noise, stretched, striking his fist painfully on the railing, and finally came round.

Then he leapt up. The lantern was gone. The stars were shining peacefully. There was the sweet scent of jasmine.

'Damn it!'

The guardsman spat so angrily that the spit flew like a bullet and knocked a jasmine bloom to the ground.

The animals' concert was thundering with growing power.

The guardsman raised the alarm. A minute later, people had come running with torches. The torches crackled. The guardsmen cursed. One got tangled up with his own sabre and fell over, breaking his nose on someone else's spur.

'I've had my lantern stolen!'

'Someone's got into the menagerie!'

'Thieves!'

'Rebels!'

The guardsman with the broken nose and a second guardsman with a broken spur, and all the rest of them too, ripped into the darkness with their torches as they moved against the unknown enemy.

But nothing suspicious was discovered in the menagerie.

The tigers roared, with their red, foul-smelling jaws gaping wide. The lions ran about in their cages in great alarm. The parrots had kicked up a real kerfuffle; they were spinning around, creating the impression of a multi-coloured carousel.

The monkeys were swinging on their trapezes. And the bears were singing in beautiful, low bass voices.

The appearance of light and people alarmed the company even more.

The guardsmen examined all the cages.

Everything was in order.

They didn't find even the lantern that Suok had dropped.

And suddenly the guardsman with the broken nose said:

'Wait!' and lifted his torch high in the air.

Everyone looked up. There, the green crown of a tree looked black. The leaves were motionless. It was a still night.

'Do you see?' the guardsman asked sternly. He gave the torch a shake.

'Yes. There's something pink…'

'Small…'

'Sitting there…'

'Idiots! Do you know what it is? It's a parrot. It's flown out of its cage and settled up there, the devil take it!'

The sentry who had raised the alarm was silent in embarrassment.

'It needs to be brought down. It's got all the animals in a state.'

'True. Up you go, Wurm. You're the youngest.'

The one who had been called Wurm went up to the tree. He hesitated.

'Climb up and pull it down by its beard.'

The parrot sat motionless. Its feathers were pink in the dense foliage, illuminated by the torch.

Wurm pulled his hat down onto his forehead and scratched the back of his head.

'I'm scared. When parrots bite, it really hurts.'

'Idiot!'

Wurm started to climb the tree nonetheless. But halfway up the trunk he stopped, held on for a second, and then slipped down.

'No way,' he said. 'It's not my job. I don't know how to fight parrots.'

At this point, the angry voice of an old man rang out. Somebody was hurrying out of the darkness towards the guardsmen, shuffling his shoes.

'There's no need to touch it!' he shouted. 'Don't disturb it!'

The man shouting turned out to be the head keeper of the menagerie.

He was a major scholar and an expert in zoology, that is, he knew absolutely everything there is to know about animals.

He had been woken by the noise.

He lived right there at the menagerie and had come running straight from his bed, without even taking off his nightcap, and even with a big shiny bedbug on his nose.

He was very excited. Well, indeed: soldiers of some sort had dared to meddle in his world, and some oaf or other meant to grab his parrot by the beard!

The guardsmen made way.

The zoologist craned his neck. He too saw something pink among the leaves.

'Yes,' he declared. 'It's a parrot. It's my best parrot. It's always throwing tantrums. It can't bear sitting in a cage. It's Laura... Laura! Laura!' he began calling in a thin little voice. 'It likes to be treated gently. Laura! Laura! Laura!'

The guardsmen chortled. In general, this little old man, wearing a coloured dressing gown, in his bedroom slippers, craning back his head, from which the tassel of his nightcap hung right down to the ground, presented an amusing spectacle in the midst of the enormous guardsmen, the brightly blazing torches and the howling of the animals.

Then the funniest thing happened. The zoologist started to climb the tree. He did it with some agility – evidently not for the first time. One, two, three! There were several quick glimpses of his legs in striped underwear under the dressing gown, and the venerable old man was up at the top, at the objective of his short, yet dangerous journey.

'Laura!' he murmured sweetly and fawningly once more.

And suddenly his piercing yell filled the menagerie, the park and the entire neighbourhood, to a distance of at least a full kilometre.

'The devil!' was what he shouted.

Instead of the parrot, there was evidently some sort of monster sitting on the branch.

The guardsmen recoiled from the tree. The zoologist was flying down. Chance, in the form of a short, but quite strong branch, saved him. He hung with his dressing gown caught on it.

Oh, if other scholars had seen their venerable colleague now, looking like this, they would, of course, have turned away out of respect for his bald patch and his knowledge! The way his dressing gown had ridden up was just too unseemly.

The guardsmen took to their heels. The flames of the torches flew in the wind. In the darkness you might have thought they were galloping black horses with fiery manes.

The alarm in the menagerie abated. The zoologist hung motionless. But in the palace there was agitation.

A quarter of an hour before the appearance of the mysterious parrot in the tree, the Three Fat Men received some unpleasant news:

'There are disturbances in town. The workers have got hold of pistols and rifles. The workers are firing at the guardsmen and throwing all the fat people into the water.'

'Tibullus the acrobat is at large and is gathering the residents of outlying districts into a single armed force.'

'Many of the guardsmen have gone off into the workers' districts so as not to continue in the service of the Three Fat Men.'

'Factory chimneys aren't smoking. Machinery's inactive. Miners are refusing to go underground after coal for the rich.'

'Peasants in surrounding areas are fighting with the owners of estates.'

That's what ministers reported to the Three Fat Men.

As usual, their alarm made the Three Fat Men start to get fatter. Before the eyes of the State Council each of them gained a quarter of a pound.

'I can't carry on!' one of them complained. 'I can't carry on... It's more than I can bear... Oh, oh! There's a stud sticking into my throat.'

And at that point his dazzling collar burst open with a crack.

'I'm getting fatter,' howled another. 'Save me!'

And the third looked dejectedly at his belly.

Thus two tasks stood before the State Council: firstly, to think of a means of stopping the fattening process at once, and secondly, to suppress the disturbances in town.

On the first question they decided the following:

'Dancing!'

'Dancing! Dancing! Yes, of course, dancing. It's the very best exercise.'

'Summon a dancing-master without a moment's delay. He must give the Three Fat Men lessons in the art of ballet.'

'Yes,' said the First Fat Man beseechingly, 'but...'

And at that very moment, from the menagerie came the cry of the respected zoologist, who had seen the devil on the branch instead of his beloved parrot, Laura.

The entire government rushed into the park and down the avenues towards the menagerie.

'Ooh! Ooh! Ooh!' could be heard in the park.

Thirty families of the very best butterflies, orange ones with black spots, left the park in terror.

A host of torches appeared. An entire burning forest that spread the smell of pitch. The forest ran and burnt.

And when there were about ten paces to go to the menagerie, it was as if all at once everything that had been running suddenly lost its legs. And everyone immediately dashed back again, howling and squealing, falling over on top of one another, rushing to and fro and trying to escape. Torches lay on the ground, flame spilled out, a wave of black smoke sped off.

'Oh!'

'Ah!'

'Flee!'

Voices rocked the park. Flames flew in all directions, lighting up the scene of flight and disarray with a crimson glow.

And from there, from the menagerie, from behind the iron railings, with long, firm strides, there calmly walked a huge man.

Red-haired, with flashing eyes, in a ripped jacket, he walked in that glow like a menacing vision. With one hand he held a panther by a collar twisted out of an iron fragment of chain. The yellow, slender animal was struggling to tear itself free of the terrible collar, jumping, yelping and twisting, and, like a lion on a knight's pennon, it was now poking out, now pulling in its long, crimson tongue.

And those who dared to look back saw that in the other arm the man was carrying a little girl in a radiant pink dress. The girl was looking at the raging panther in fright, drawing up her feet in their shoes with pink roses and pressing against the shoulder of her friend.

'Prospero!' the people shrieked as they ran for it.

'Prospero! It's Prospero!'

'Flee!'

'The doll!'

'The doll!'

And then Prospero let the animal go.

Waving its tail around and with huge bounds, the panther dashed after the fleeing people.

Suok leapt down from the armourer's arm. A lot of pistols had been thrown down onto the grass during the flight. Suok picked up three pistols. Prospero armed himself with two of them, and Suok took one. It was almost half as big as she was. But she knew how to handle this black, shiny object: she had learnt to shoot a pistol in the circus.

'Let's go!' the armourer commanded.

They weren't interested in what was going on in the depths of the park. They didn't think about the further adventures of the panther.

They had to look for the way out of the palace. They had to escape.

Where was the clandestine saucepan that Tibullus had spoken of? Where was the secret saucepan through which the children's balloon seller had escaped?

'To the kitchen! To the kitchen!' cried Suok as she went, brandishing the pistol.

She was running in total darkness, tearing bushes apart and driving out sleeping birds. Oh, how Suok's wonderful dress suffered!

'There's a smell of something sweet,' Suok suddenly declared, stopping beneath some lighted windows.

And instead of the finger which people raise in instances when general attention is required, she raised the black pistol.

The guardsmen who came running saw them when they were already up at the top of the tree. Another instant, and they had climbed across from the boughs stretched out towards the windows into the main one.

It was that same window through which the children's balloon seller had flown in the day before.

It was the window of the confectionary.

There, in spite of the late hour, and even in spite of the general alarm, work was in full swing. The entire complement of confectioners and cunning little boys in white caps was bustling about like anything: they were preparing a special sort of stewed fruit for lunch the following day in honour of the return of Tutti the Heir's doll. It had already been decided not to make a cake this time for fear that some other flying guest might ruin both the French butter cream and the amazingly high-quality candied peel.

In the middle stood a vat. Water was being boiled in it. Everything was clouded in white steam. Under this blanket the kitchen-lads were in a state of bliss: they were cutting up the fruit for stewing.

And so... But here, through the steam and the commotion, the chefs saw a terrifying picture.

Outside the window, boughs swayed and leaves rustled, as if before a storm, and two figures appeared on the window ledge: a red-haired giant and a little girl.

'Hands up!' said Prospero. In each hand he held a pistol.

'Don't move!' said Suok in a ringing voice, raising her pistol.

Two dozen white sleeves flung themselves up into the air without waiting for a more forcible invitation.

And then the saucepans went flying.

This was the demolition of the glittering glass, copper, hot, sweet, fragrant world of the confectionary.

The armourer was searching for the most important sauce-pan. Inside it was his salvation and the salvation of his little saviour.

He was overturning jars, throwing frying-pans, funnels, plates and dishes around. Glass was flying in all directions and breaking with a ringing and a crashing; there was a twisting column of spilled flour like a simoom in the Sahara; there rose a whirlwind of almonds, currants, cherries; granulated sugar streamed from the shelves with the din of a waterfall; a flood of syrup rose to a depth of a whole foot; water splashed, fruits rolled around, copper towers of saucepans collapsed. Everything was upside down. It's like that when you're asleep sometimes, when you're having a dream and you know that it's a dream, and so you can do whatever you want.

'Got it!' squealed Suok. 'Here it is!'

They had found what they were looking for. The lid flew into a pile of debris. It plopped into a thick, crimson, green and golden-yellow lake of syrup.

Prospero saw the bottomless saucepan.

'Run!' cried Suok. 'I'll follow you!'

The armourer climbed into the saucepan. And when he had already disappeared inside, he heard the howling of those who remained in the confectionary.

Suok wasn't in time. The panther, concluding its terrible journey through the park and the palace, had appeared there. Wounds made by guardsmen's bullets were flowering on its hide like roses.

The confectioners and cooks fell into one corner. Suok, forgetting about the pistol, flung a pear which was to hand at the panther.

The animal threw itself after Prospero, headfirst into the saucepan. It tumbled down after him into the dark and narrow passage. Everyone saw a yellow tail poking out of the saucepan, as though out of a well. And then everything disappeared.

Suok covered her eyes with her hands.

'Prospero! Prospero!'

But the confectioners set up a sinister chuckling. Some guardsmen burst in at once. Their uniforms were ripped, their faces were bloody, their pistols were smoking. They had been fighting with the panther.

'Prospero's done for! The panther will tear him apart! I don't care then. I surrender.' Suok spoke calmly, and her little hand with the very large pistol hung down.

But a shot rang out. It was Prospero, escaping down the underground passage, shooting at the panther flying after him.

The guardsmen clustered over the saucepan. The syrup lake came halfway up their enormous boots.

One of them looked into the saucepan. Then he put in his arm and pulled. And then two more came to his aid. Straining, they pulled the dead animal, which had got stuck in the funnel, out by the tail.

'He's dead,' said the guardsman, puffing hard.

'He's alive! He's alive! I've saved him. I've saved the people's friend!'

That's how Suok rejoiced, poor little Suok, in a tattered little dress, with crumpled golden roses in her hair and on her shoes.

She was pink with happiness.

She had carried out the mission that her friend, Tibullus the acrobat, had given her: she had freed Prospero the armourer.

'Right!' said a guardsman, taking Suok by the arm. 'Let's see what you're going to do now, O exalted doll! Let's see...'

'Take her to the Three Fat Men...'

'They'll condemn you to death.'

'Idiot,' Suok replied calmly, licking off a sweet blob of syrup which had got onto the pink lace of her dress when Prospero had been demolishing the confectionary.

Onetwothreesir The Dancing-Master

What happened to the doll next, after she had been exposed, is, for the moment, unknown. What's more, we shall refrain for the time being from other explanations too, namely: exactly which parrot it was sitting in the tree, and what it was that the venerable zoologist – who may still be hanging from the branch like a laundered shirt – was so frightened about; how Prospero the armourer came to be free, and where the panther appeared from; by what means Suok came to be on the armourer's shoulder; what the monster that spoke in human language was, what the little board it gave to Suok was, and why it died…

All will be clarified in good time. I can assure you that there were no miracles, and everything happened, as scholars put it, in accordance with the iron laws of logic.

But now it was morning. And nature had become amazingly beautiful right on cue for that morning. Even an old maid with the expressive appearance of a goat found that her head, which had ached since she was a child, had stopped hurting. Such was the air that morning. The trees didn't rustle, but rather sang in the merry voices of children.

On such a morning everyone feels like dancing. It's no wonder, then, that the dancing-master Onetwothreesir's hall was overcrowded.

Of course, you can't dance on an empty stomach. Nor can you dance, of course, when you're grief-stricken. But the only ones with empty stomachs and grief were those preparing that day in the workers' districts to march once more on the Palace of the Three Fat Men. And the dandies, the ladies, the sons and daughters of the gluttonous and rich felt marvellous. They didn't know that Tibullus the acrobat was forming the poor, hungry, working people into regiments; they didn't know that the little dancer Suok had freed Prospero the armourer, who was all that the people were waiting for; they attached little significance to the unrest that had sprung up in town.

'It's nothing!' said a pretty, but sharp-nosed young lady, preparing her dancing shoes. 'If they go and storm the palace again, the guardsmen will annihilate them like last time.'

'Of course!' a young dandy broke in, gnawing an apple and examining his tailcoat. 'Those miners and those filthy artisans have no rifles, pistols or sabres, whereas the guardsmen even have cannons.'

One after another, carefree and self-satisfied couples approached Onetwothreesir's house.

On his door hung a plate with the inscription:

Dancing-master Onetwothreesir.
I teach not only dancing,
but beauty, elegance, grace, courtesy
and a poetic outlook on life.
Payment in advance for ten dances.

In a circular hall, on a large parquet floor the colour of honey, Onetwothreesir taught his art.

He himself played a black flute, which remained at his lips by some sort of miracle, because he would be waving his hands around all the time in their lacy cuffs and white kid gloves. He contorted himself into striking poses, he rolled his eyes as he beat time with his heel, and he was constantly running to the mirror to see whether he looked handsome, whether his bows were properly in place, and whether his pomaded hair was shining...

Couples were spinning around. There were so many of them and they were sweating so, you might have thought that some motley and probably vile-tasting soup was on the boil.

Spinning around in the general hurly-burly, first a gentleman, then a lady would start to resemble either a long-tailed turnip, or a cabbage leaf, or something else unrecognisable, coloured and peculiar that might be found in a bowl of soup.

And in this bowl of soup, Onetwothreesir performed the duties of the spoon, and rightly so, as he was very tall, slender and curved.

Ah, if Suok had taken a look at this dancing, how she would have laughed! Even when she had played the part of the Golden Cabbage-stalk in the pantomime *The Foolish King*, even then she had danced much more elegantly, despite having had to dance the way that cabbage-stalks do.

And at the very height of the dancing, three huge fists in rough leather gloves banged on Onetwothreesir the dancing-master's door.

Those gloves were scarcely distinguishable in appearance from rural clay jugs.

The soup stopped.

And five minutes later, Onetwothreesir the dancing-master was being taken to the Palace of the Three Fat Men. Three guardsmen had come galloping to fetch him. One of them sat him on the crupper of his horse with his back towards him – in other words, Onetwothreesir rode back to front. Another of the guardsmen carried his big cardboard box. It was most capacious.

'After all, I have to take costumes with me, musical instruments, and also wigs, sheet music and favourite romances,' declared Onetwothreesir as he got ready to go. 'Who knows how long I might have to stay at the palace. And I'm accustomed to elegance and beauty, so I enjoy a frequent change of clothes.'

The dancers ran after the horses, waved their handkerchiefs and called out salutations to Onetwothreesir.

The sun had climbed high.

Onetwothreesir was glad that he had been summoned to the palace: he liked the Three Fat Men because they were liked by the sons and daughters of the no less fat and rich. The richer a rich man was, the more Onetwothreesir liked him.

'Indeed,' he reasoned, 'what use are the poor to me? Do they learn to dance? They're always busy working and never have any money. But rich merchants, rich dandies and ladies are quite another matter! They always have a lot of money, and they never do anything.'

As you can see, the way *he* understood things, Onetwothreesir wasn't foolish, but the way *we* understand them, he was.

'She's an idiot, that Suok,' he marvelled, remembering the little dancer. 'Why does she dance for beggars, for soldiers, artisans and ragged children? After all, they pay her so little money.'

Foolish Onetwothreesir would probably have marvelled still more if he had learnt that the little dancer had risked her life to save the leader of those beggars, artisans and ragged children – Prospero the armourer.

The horsemen went at a fast gallop.

There were some quite strange occurrences on the way. Shots were constantly being fired in the distance. Knots of excited people were crowding by their gates. Two or three artisans holding pistols in their hands would sometimes run across the street... You would have thought the shopkeepers would have done nothing but trade on such a wonderful day, but they were closing their windows and poking their fat, shiny cheeks out of the transoms. Different voices exchanged calls from one block to another:

'Prospero!'

'Prospero!'

'He's with us!'

'Wi-ith us!'

At times a guardsman would fly past on an excited horse spraying out lather. At times a fat man would run panting into a lane, while ran on either side of him ginger-haired servants with sticks at the ready to defend their gentleman.

In one spot, instead of defending their fat master, such servants quite unexpectedly set about beating him up, making enough noise for the whole block to hear.

Onetwothreesir thought at first they were beating the dust out of a Turkish divan.

After dishing out three dozen blows, the servants took it in turns to give the fat man a kick in the backside, then, with their arms round each other and shaking their sticks, they ran off somewhere, shouting:

'Down with the Three Fat Men! We don't want to work for the rich! Long live the people!'

And voices exchanged calls:

'Prospero!'

'Pro-o-ospe-ero!'

In a word, there was great alarm. There was the smell of gunpowder in the air.

And finally there was the last occurrence.

Ten guardsmen blocked the path of their three comrades conveying Onetwothreesir. They were foot guards.

'Halt!' said one of them. There was a flash of anger in his blue eyes. 'Who are you?'

'Can't you see?!' asked the guardsman behind whose back sat Onetwothreesir, and just as angrily.

The horses, stopped at full speed, couldn't stand still. Their harnesses were shaking. And Onetwothreesir the dancing-master was shaking in his shoes. It's uncertain which shaking was the louder.

'We're soldiers of the Palace Guard of the Three Fat Men.'

'We're hurrying to the palace. Let us through at once.'

Then the blue-eyed guardsman drew a pistol from under his scarf and said:

'In that case, hand over your pistols and sabres. A soldier's weapons should serve only the people, and not the Three Fat Men.'

All the guardsmen surrounding the horsemen drew their pistols.

The horsemen went for their weapons. Onetwothreesir fainted away and fell off the horse. Exactly when he came round is impossible to say, but it was, in any event, after the end of the battle between the guardsmen who had been escorting him and the ones who had stopped them. The latter had evidently won. Next to him, Onetwothreesir saw the guardsman behind whose back he had been sitting. He was dead.

'Blood,' murmured Onetwothreesir, closing his eyes.

But what he saw a second later shook him three times as badly.

His cardboard box was smashed. His belongings had fallen out of the wreckage of the box. His wonderful clothes, his romances and wigs were lying about on the roadway in the dust.

'Oh dear!…'

In the heat of the engagement the guardsman had dropped the box which had been entrusted to him, and it had smashed on the stones of the roadway.

'Oh dear! Oh!'

Onetwothreesir threw himself upon his property. He looked feverishly through the waistcoats, tailcoats and stockings, the shoes with cheap, but at first glance handsome buckles, and sat down again on the ground. His grief knew no bounds. All his things, his entire toilet was still in place, but the most important thing had been stolen.

And while Onetwothreesir was lifting his little fists that looked like bread rolls up to the blue sky, three horsemen were hurtling at full tilt towards the Palace of the Three Fat Men.

Before the engagement, their horses had belonged to the three guardsmen conveying Onetwothreesir the dancing-master. After the engagement, when one of them had been killed and the others had surrendered and gone over to the side of the people, in Onetwothreesir's smashed box the victors had found something pink and wrapped in gauze.

Then three of them had immediately leapt onto the horses they had captured and galloped off.

The blue-eyed guardsman galloping in front was pressing something pink and wrapped in gauze to his chest.

The people he met jumped aside. The guardsman had a red cockade on his hat. That meant he had gone over to the side of the people.

Then, if they weren't fat men and gluttons, the people he met applauded in his wake. But upon looking closer, they froze in astonishment: hanging down from the bundle which the guardsman was holding at his breast were the feet of a little girl in pink shoes with gold roses instead of buckles…

Victory

We have just been describing the morning and its extraordinary occurrences, but now we shall turn back and describe the night which preceded that morning and which was, as you already know, filled with occurrences no less amazing.

That night, Prospero the armourer escaped from the Palace of the Three Fat Men; that night, Suok was seized at the scene of the crime.

What's more, that night, three men with screened lanterns entered the bedroom of Tutti the Heir.

This happened approximately an hour after Prospero the armourer demolished the palace confectionary and the guardsmen took Suok prisoner beside the escape saucepan.

It was dark in the bedroom.

The tall windows were filled with stars.

The boy was fast asleep, breathing very peacefully and quietly.

The three men tried in every possible way to hide the light of their lanterns.

What they were doing is unknown. Only whispering could be heard. The sentry, standing outside by the bedroom doors, continued to stand there as if nothing were wrong.

The trio who had gone into the Heir's room evidently had some sort of right to treat his bedroom as if they owned it.

You already know that Tutti the Heir's tutors weren't noted for their bravery. You remember the incident with the doll. You remember how frightened the tutor was at the terrible scene in the garden when the guardsmen stabbed the doll with their sabres. You saw how cowardly the tutor was when telling the Three Fat Men about that scene.

On this occasion the tutor on duty proved to be just such a coward.

Imagine, he was in the bedroom when the three unknown men came in with their lanterns. He was sitting by the window, watching over the Heir's sleep, and, so as not to nod off, he was looking at the stars and testing his knowledge of astronomy.

But at that point, the door creaked, there was a flash of light and a glimpse of three mysterious figures. Then the tutor hid in the armchair. Most of all he was scared that his long nose would give him away. That amazing nose was, indeed, distinct and black against the background of the starry window and could be spotted at once.

But the coward tried to reassure himself: 'Perhaps they'll think it's some sort of decoration on the arm of the chair, or a ledge on the building opposite.'

The three figures, faintly illuminated by the yellow light of the lanterns, went up to the Heir's bed.

'He's here,' came a whisper.

'He's asleep,' replied another.

'Ssh!...'

'It's all right. He's fast asleep.'

'So, to work.'

Something tinkled.

Cold sweat broke out on the tutor's forehead. He felt as if fear were making his nose grow.

'It's ready,' hissed somebody's voice.

'Come on then.'

Again something tinkled, then gave a glug and began pouring. And suddenly quietness fell again.

'Where shall I pour it?'

'Into his ear.'

'He's sleeping on one cheek. Couldn't be more convenient. Pour it into his ear...'

'Carefully, though. One drop at a time.'

'Exactly ten drops.'

'The first drop seems terribly cold, but the second causes no sensation, because the first one acts instantly. After it, all sensitivity disappears.'

'Try to pour the liquid in so that there's no gap at all between the first drop and the second.'

'Otherwise the boy'll wake up, as though he's been touched by ice.'

'Ssh!... I'm pouring... Onc, two!...'

And at that point the tutor noticed a strong smell of lily of the valley. It spread throughout the room.

'Three, four, five, six...' somebody's voice counted out in a rapid whisper.

'That's it.'

'He'll be in a deep sleep for three days now.'

'And he won't know what's happened to his doll...'

'He'll wake up when everything's all over.'

'Otherwise he might have started crying and stamping his feet, and in the end the Three Fat Men would have forgiven the girl and granted her her life...'

The three unknown men disappeared. The trembling tutor got up. He lit a little lamp, which burnt with a flame in the shape of an orange flower, and went up to the bed.

Tutti the Heir lay in lace beneath silk coverlets, small and grand.

Resting on enormous pillows was his head with its tousled golden hair.

The tutor bent down and brought the lamp close to the boy's pale face. A drop of liquid was glistening in his little ear like a pearl in a shell.

A gold-green light was playing in it. The tutor touched it with his little finger. Nothing remained on the ear, but an acute, unbearable coldness flooded through the tutor's entire arm.

The boy was in a deep sleep.

But a few hours later, the delightful morning we have already had the pleasure of describing to our readers dawned.

We know what happened that morning to the dancing-master Onetwothreesir, but much more interesting for us is to find out what became of Suok that morning. After all, we left her in such an awful situation!

First of all it was decided to throw her into a dungeon.

'No, that's too complicated,' said the State Chancellor. 'We'll hold a quick and fair trial.'

'Of course, there's no point in taking a lot of trouble over the girl,' the Three Fat Men agreed.

Don't forget, however, that the Three Fat Men had gone through some very unpleasant moments when getting away from the panther. It was essential they had a rest. This is what they said:

'We'll have a little sleep. And in the morning we'll hold the trial.'

With these words they dispersed to their bedrooms.

The State Chancellor, who was in no doubt that the doll which had turned out to be a little girl would be sentenced to capital punishment by the court, gave the order for Tutti the Heir to be put to sleep so that he didn't reduce the terrible sentence with his tears.

The three men with lanterns, as you already know, carried this out.

Tutti the Heir was asleep.

Suok was sitting in the sentries' room. The sentries' room is called the guardhouse. And so, that morning, Suok was sitting in the guardhouse. She was surrounded by guardsmen. An outsider coming into the guardhouse would have wondered for a long time why this pretty, sad little girl in the unusually smart pink dress was here among the guardsmen. Her appearance wasn't at all in keeping with the rough setting of the guardhouse, where saddles, weapons and beer-mugs were all lying around.

The guardsmen were playing cards, giving out foul-smelling blue smoke from their pipes, cursing, and continually starting fights.

These guardsmen were still loyal to the Three Fat Men. They shook their huge fists at Suok, pulled ugly faces and stamped their feet at her.

Suok took it calmly. To rid herself of their attention and to spite them, she stuck her tongue out and, turning to them all at once, she sat with her face like that for a whole hour.

Sitting on a keg seemed to her comfortable enough. True, the seat was making her dress dirty, but it had lost its former appearance anyway: it had been ripped by branches, singed by torches, crumpled by guardsmen, splattered with syrup.

Suok wasn't thinking about her fate. Girls of her age aren't afraid of obvious danger. They aren't frightened by a pistol barrel being aimed at them, yet at the same time they're scared of being left alone in a dark room.

This is what she was thinking: 'Prospero the armourer is at large. With Tibullus, he'll soon be leading the poor people to the palace. They'll set me free.'

At the time Suok was reflecting thus, up to the palace galloped the three guardsmen we were talking about in the last chapter. One of them, the blue-eyed one, was carrying, as you know, some mysterious bundle, from which hung feet in pink shoes with gold roses instead of buckles.

Riding up to a bridge where there were sentries loyal to the Three Fat Men, these three guardsmen tore the red cockades from their hats.

This was essential so that the sentries would let them pass.

Otherwise, if the sentries had seen the red cockades, they would have begun firing on those guardsmen because they had gone over to the side of the people.

They hurtled past the sentries, almost knocking their commander over.

'Must be some important dispatch,' said the commander, picking up his hat and brushing the dust from his uniform.

At that moment, Suok's final hour had come. The State Chancellor had entered the guardhouse.

The guardsmen leapt up and stood to attention, stretching their huge gloves down along the seams of their trousers.

'Where's the girl?' asked the Chancellor, lifting up his glasses.

'Come here!' shouted the chief guardsman to the little girl.

Suok slid down from the keg.

The guardsman grabbed her roughly round the waist and lifted her up.

'The Three Fat Men are waiting in the Courtroom,' said the Chancellor, lowering his glasses. 'Follow me with the girl.'

With these words the Chancellor left the guardhouse. The guardsman strode after him with Suok suspended on one arm.

Oh, the gold roses! Oh, the pink silk! It was all being ruined by that pitiless arm.

Suok, who found it painful and uncomfortable hanging over the guardsman's terrible arm, pinched him just above the elbow. She had gathered her strength, and the pinch was a hard one, despite the thick sleeve of his uniform.

'Damn!' the guardsman cursed and dropped the girl.

'What?' asked the Chancellor, turning.

And at that point the Chancellor felt a completely unexpected blow on the ear. The Chancellor fell down.

And the guardsman who had just been dealing with Suok fell down immediately after him.

He had been struck on the ear as well. And how! You can imagine how hard a blow has to be to knock such a huge and fierce guardsman senseless!

Before Suok had had time to look around, somebody's hands picked her up again and hauled her off.

These hands too were rough and strong, but they seemed kinder, and Suok felt more comfortable in them than in the hands of the guardsman who now lay on the shiny floor.

'Don't be afraid!' someone's voice whispered to her.

The Fat Men were waiting impatiently in the Courtroom. They wanted to try the cunning doll themselves. All around sat officials, advisers, judges and secretaries. Wigs of many colours – crimson, lilac, bright-green, ginger, white and gold – glowed in the sun's rays. But even the cheerful sunlight couldn't brighten up the haughty physiognomies beneath those wigs.

The Three Fat Men were suffering, as ever, from the heat. Sweat was pouring off them in streams and spoiling the sheets of paper that lay in front of them. Secretaries were continually changing the paper.

'Our Chancellor is keeping us waiting a long time,' said the First Fat Man, jerking his fingers like someone being strangled.

Those so long awaited finally appeared.

Three guardsmen entered the room. One was holding a little girl in his arms. Oh, how sad she looked!

The pink dress, which the day before had been striking in its radiance and expensive, expert finish, had by now turned into pitiful rags. The gold roses had withered, the sequins had fallen off, the silk was crumpled and torn. The girl's head hung dejectedly against the guardsman's shoulder. The girl was deathly pale, and her mischievous grey eyes had lost their light.

The motley assembly lifted their heads.

The Three Fat Men rubbed their hands.

The secretaries took long quills from behind their no-less-long ears.

'So,' said the First Fat Man. 'Where's the State Chancellor?'

The guardsman who was holding the girl stood before the assembly and, with his blue eyes shining merrily, reported:

'The State Chancellor got a stomach upset on the way.'

This explanation satisfied everyone.

The trial began.

The guardsman sat the poor little girl down on a rough bench in front of the judges' table. She sat with her head hanging.

The First Fat Man began the questioning.

But at this point a most important obstacle was encountered. Suok didn't want to answer a single question.

'Splendid!' said the Fat Man angrily. 'Splendid. It'll be the worse for her. If she doesn't honour us with an answer – fine. The more terrible the punishment we'll come up with for her!'

Suok didn't stir.

The three guardsmen stood on either side as if turned to stone.

'Call the witnesses!' ordered the Fat Man.

There was only one witness. He was led in. It was the respected zoologist, the keeper of the menagerie. He had been hanging on the branch all night. Only now had he been taken down. And that's just how he came in: wearing the coloured dressing gown, the striped underwear and the nightcap. The tassel on the nightcap dragged across the floor behind him like a hose.

Upon seeing Suok, who was sitting on the bench, the zoologist began to sway in terror. He was given support.

'Tell us what happened.'

The zoologist set about giving a detailed account. He reported how, after climbing up into the tree, between the branches he had seen Tutti the Heir's doll. Since he had never seen any living dolls and hadn't supposed that dolls climbed trees at night, he had been very frightened and had fainted.

'How did she free Prospero the armourer?'

'I don't know. I didn't see and I didn't hear. My faint was a very deep one.'

'Will you answer us, you vile little girl: how did Prospero the armourer come to be free?'

Suok was silent.

'Give her a shake.'

'A good one!' the Fat Men ordered.

The blue-eyed guardsman shook the little girl by the shoulders. What's more, he gave her a really painful flick on the forehead.

Suok was silent.

The Fat Men began to hiss with rage. The multi-coloured heads began shaking reproachfully.

'We evidently won't succeed,' said the First Fat Man, 'in learning any of the details.'

At these words the zoologist struck himself on the forehead with the palm of his hand.

'I know what needs to be done!'

The assembly pricked up their ears.

'In the menagerie there's a cage of parrots. The rarest breeds of parrot are assembled there. You're aware, of course, that parrots are able to remember and repeat human speech. Many parrots have wonderful hearing and a magnificent memory... I expect they remember everything that was done in the menagerie in the night by this girl and Prospero the armourer... And so I propose summoning one of my wonderful parrots to the Courtroom as a witness.'

A hum of approval ran through the assembly.

The zoologist set off for the menagerie and soon returned. On his index finger sat the large old parrot with the long red beard.

Remember: when Suok was wandering through the menagerie in the night – remember! – one of the parrots seemed suspicious to her. You remember, she saw how he looked at her and, pretending to be asleep, smiled into his long red beard.

And now, on the zoologist's finger, just as comfortably as on its silver perch, there sat that very same red-bearded parrot.

Now it was smiling most unambiguously, rejoicing that it would be giving poor Suok away.

The zoologist began speaking to it in German. The little girl was shown to the parrot.

Then it flapped its wings and cried,

'Suok! Suok!'

Its voice was like the creaking of an old gate which the wind is tearing off its rusty hinges.

The assembly was silent.

The zoologist was triumphant.

And the parrot continued making its denunciation. It did, indeed, tell what it had heard in the night. So if you're interested in the story of the liberation of Prospero the armourer, listen to everything the parrot cries out.

Oh, it really was a rare breed of parrot. Quite apart from the beautiful red beard, which would have done any general proud, the parrot conveyed human speech in the most skilled manner.

'Who are you?' it creaked in a male voice.

And at once it replied very shrilly, imitating the voice of a little girl:

'I'm Suok.'

'Suok!'

'Tibullus sent me. I'm not a doll. I'm a living girl. I've come to set you free. Didn't you see me come into the menagerie?'

'No. I think I was asleep. I fell asleep for the first time today.'

'I've been looking for you in the menagerie. I saw a monster here that spoke with a human voice. I thought it was you. The monster's dead.'

'That's Toob. So he's dead, then?'

'Yes. I was frightened and cried out. The guardsmen came and I hid up a tree. I'm so glad you're alive! I've come to set you free.'

'My cage is locked up tight.'

'I've got the key to your cage.'

When the parrot squawked out the last phrase, everyone was filled with indignation.

'Oh, you villainous girl!' the Fat Men yelled. 'Everything's clear now. She stole the key from Tutti the Heir and let the armourer out. The armourer snapped his chain, broke open the panther's cage and seized the animal so as to pass freely through the courtyard.'

'Yes!'

'Yes!'

'Yes!'

But Suok was silent.

The parrot gave an affirmative nod of its beard and flapped its wings thrice.

The trial ended. This was the sentence:

'The sham doll tricked Tutti the Heir. She let out the chief rebel and enemy of the Three Fat Men – Prospero the armourer. Because of her, the best specimen of panther was killed. And so the trickster is sentenced to death. She is to be torn apart by wild animals.'

And just imagine: even when the sentence had been read out, Suok didn't stir!

The entire assembly moved to the menagerie. The procession was greeted by the howling, squealing and whistling of the animals. More excited than anyone was the zoologist: after all, he was the keeper of the menagerie!

The Three Fat Men, the advisers, the officials and other courtiers took up their positions on a platform. It was protected by railings.

Ah, how gently the sun shone! Ah, how blue was the sky! How the parrots' capes gleamed, how the monkeys spun around, how the greenish elephant danced!

Poor Suok! She didn't admire any of this. She must have been looking with eyes filled with horror at the dirty cage where the tigers were cowering and running around. They looked like wasps – at least, they had the same colouring: yellow with brown stripes.

They looked from under their brows at the people. Sometimes, noiselessly, they would open wide their scarlet jaws, from which came the stench of raw meat.

Poor Suok!

Farewell the circus, the squares, Augustus, the fox in the cage, dear, big, bold Tibullus!

The blue-eyed guardsman carried the little girl out into the centre of the menagerie and laid her down on the shining hot graphite.

'Forgive me,' said one of the advisers all of a sudden. 'But what about Tutti the Heir? I mean, if he finds out that his doll has perished in the clutches of the tigers, he'll cry himself to death.'

'Ssh!' his neighbour whispered to him. 'Ssh! Tutti the Heir has been put to sleep... He'll be in a deep sleep for three days, or maybe even longer...'

All eyes were fixed upon the pitiful little pink ball that lay in the circle between the cages.

Then the animal-tamer made his entry, cracking his whip and with his pistol flashing. The musicians struck up a march. And thus Suok appeared before the public for the last time.

'*Allez*!' cried the tamer.

The iron door of a cage made a rattling noise. Heavily and noiselessly, the tigers ran out of the cage.

The Fat Men started chuckling. The advisers started giggling and shaking their wigs. The whip cracked.

The three tigers ran up to Suok.

She lay motionless, gazing into the sky with motionless grey eyes. Everyone half rose. Everyone was ready to cry out in pleasure on seeing the animals mete out punishment to the little friend of the people...

But... the tigers approached, one bent its big-browed head down and took a sniff, another touched the little girl with a feline paw, the third paid no attention at all, ran on by and, stopping in front of the platform, began growling at the Fat Men.

Then everyone saw that it wasn't a living girl, but a doll – a torn, old, good-for-nothing doll.

There was utter pandemonium. In his embarrassment, the zoologist bit off half of his tongue. The tamer drove the animals back into the cage and, tossing the dead doll up contemptuously with his foot, he left to take off his ceremonial dress, dark-blue with gold braid.

The company was silent for five minutes.

And the silence was broken in the most unexpected manner: in the blue sky above the menagerie a bomb exploded.

All the spectators crashed nose-down onto the wooden floor of the platform. All the animals stood up on their hind legs. At once a second bomb exploded. The sky filled with white, round puffs of smoke.

'What is it? What is it? What is it?' the cries flew.

'The people are coming in for the assault!'

'The people have cannons!'

'The guardsmen have betrayed us!'

'Oh! Ah!! Oh!!!'

The park was filled with noise, cries and shots. The rebels had broken into the park – that was clear!

The whole company hurried to flee from the menagerie. The ministers drew their swords. The Fat Men yelled blue murder.

In the park they saw the following.

People were advancing from all directions. There was a multitude of them. Bared heads, bloodied brows, ripped jackets, happy faces... It was the people who that day had won the victory. Guardsmen were mingling with them. Red cockades were shining on their caps. The workers were armed as well. A whole army of the poor in brown clothes and wooden shoes was drawing near. Trees bent under the pressure of them and bushes cracked.

'We've won!' cried the people.

The Three Fat Men saw there was no escape.

'No!' one of them howled. 'It's not true! Guardsmen, fire at them!'

But the guardsmen were standing in the same ranks as the poor. And then there thundered out a voice which drowned the noise of the whole crowd. It was Prospero the armourer speaking.

'Surrender! The people have won. The reign of the rich and the gluttonous is over. The whole town is in the hands of the people. All the Fat Men have been captured.'

A solid, multi-coloured, excitable wall surrounded the Fat Men.

The people were waving scarlet banners, sticks and sabres and shaking their fists. And at this point a song was begun.

Tibullus, in his green cape, his head bandaged with a cloth through which the blood was oozing, stood alongside Prospero.

'This is a dream!' cried one of the Fat Men, covering his eyes with his hands.

Tibullus and Prospero had started singing. Thousands took up the song. It flew across the whole huge park, over the canals and bridges. The people advancing towards the palace from the town gates heard it and began to sing too. The song rolled like an ocean wave down the road, through the gates, into the town, down all the streets where the workers and the poor were advancing. And now the whole town was singing this song. It was the song of a people who had defeated their oppressors.

The Three Fat Men and their ministers, taken unawares in the palace, were not the only ones to cringe, to shrink, to huddle into a pitiful herd at the sounds of that song – all the dandies in town, the fat shopkeepers, the gluttons, the merchants, the grand ladies, the bald generals fled in fear and confusion, as though these weren't the words of a song, but shots and fire.

They looked for places to hide, they plugged their ears, they buried their heads in expensive embroidered pillows.

It ended with a huge crowd of the rich running to the harbour to board boats and sail away from the country where they had lost everything: their power, their money and the free-and-easy life of the idle. But there they were surrounded by sailors. The rich were arrested. They asked for forgiveness. They said:

'Don't harm us! We won't force you to work for us any more…'

But the people didn't believe them, because the rich had deceived the poor and the workers more than once before.

The sun was high above the town. The clear sky was blue. You might have thought that a great, unprecedented public holiday was being celebrated.

Everything was in the hands of the people: the arsenals, the barracks, the palaces, the grain warehouses, the shops. Everywhere guardsmen stood on watch with red cockades on their hats.

Scarlet flags fluttered at crossroads with the inscriptions:

> *All that is made by the hands of the poor*
> *Belongs to the poor!*
> *Long live the people!*
> *Down with the idlers and gluttons!*

But what happened to the Three Fat Men?

They were taken to the main hall of the palace to be shown to the people. Workers in grey jackets with green cuffs, their guns held horizontal, made up the escort. The hall sparkled with thousands of sun-blinks. So many people were there! But how different this gathering was to the one before which little Suok had sung on the day she met Tutti the Heir!

Here were all the spectators who used to applaud her in squares and at markets. But now their faces seemed cheerful and happy. People crowded together, climbed onto one another's backs, laughed and joked. Some cried with joy.

Never had the ceremonial halls of the palace seen such guests. And never before had the sun lit them so brightly.

'Ssh!'

'Quiet!'

'Quiet!'

A procession of prisoners appeared at the top of the staircase. The Three Fat Men were looking down at the ground. In front walked Prospero, and with him Tibullus.

The columns rocked at the rapturous cries, and the Three Fat Men were deafened. They were led down the staircase so that the people could get a closer look at them and be sure that they had those terrible Fat Men in captivity.

'Here,' said Prospero, standing by a column.

He was almost half the height of that enormous column, and his red hair burnt with an unendurable flame in the radiance of the sun.

'Here,' he said, 'here are the Three Fat Men. They crushed the poor people. They forced us to work until we sweated blood, and they took everything away from us. See how fat they've grown! We have defeated them. Now we shall work for ourselves, we shall all be equal. We shan't have any rich men, or idlers, or gluttons. Then things will go well for us, we shall all be well-fed and rich. And should they go badly for us, then we shall know that there's no one growing fat while we go hungry…'

'Hurrah! Hurrah!' came the cries.

The Three Fat Men huffed and puffed.

'Today is the day of our victory. Look how the sun is shining! Listen to the way the birds are singing! Smell the scent of the flowers! Remember this day, remember this hour!'

And when the word 'hour' rang out, all heads turned to where the clock was.

It hung between two columns in a deep niche. There was a huge case made of oak with carving and enamel decoration. In the middle was a dark disc with the figures on it.

'What's the time?' everyone thought.

And suddenly (and now this is the last 'suddenly' in our novel)… suddenly the oak door of the case opened up. There turned out to be no mechanism within. The entire movement of the clock had been ripped out. And instead of brass wheels and springs, inside the cabinet there sat a pink, sparkling and radiant Suok.

'Suok!' the hall sighed.

'Suok!' shouted the children.

'Suok! Suok! Suok!'

There was thunderous applause.

A blue-eyed guardsman took the little girl out of the cabinet. It was the same blue-eyed guardsman who had carried off Tutti the Heir's doll from the cardboard box of Onetwothreesir the dancing-master. He had brought it to the palace, and with a blow of his fist he had felled the State Chancellor and then the guardsman who had been lugging poor, living Suok. He had hidden Suok in the clock cabinet and put the dead, tattered doll in her place. You remember how he shook the stuffed creature by the shoulders in the Courtroom and how he gave it up to be torn to pieces by the wild animals?

The little girl was passed from hand to hand. The people who had called her the best dancer in the world, the people who had thrown their last coins onto the rug for her, took her in their arms, whispered 'Suok!', kissed her, squeezed her to their breasts. There, beneath rough, torn jackets covered in soot and tar, beat hearts worn out by suffering, but that were big and full of tenderness.

She laughed, patted their tangled hair, wiped the fresh blood from their faces with her little hands, tugged at the children and pulled faces at them, cried and babbled something incomprehensible.

'Give her here,' said Prospero the armourer in a quavering voice; it seemed to many that tears shone in his eyes. 'She's my saviour!'

'Over here! Over here!' cried Tibullus, waving his green cape around like a huge burdock leaf. 'She's my little friend. Come here, Suok!'

And hurrying from a long way off, forcing his way through the crowd, came little, smiling Dr Gaspar.

The Three Fat Men were herded into that same cage in which Prospero the armourer had been held.

Epilogue

A year later there was a noisy and merry public holiday. The people were celebrating the first anniversary of liberation from the rule of the Three Fat Men.

A show had been organised for the children in Star Circus.

Vividly inscribed on the posters was:

SUOK! SUOK! SUOK!

Thousands of children awaited the appearance of their favourite actress. And on this festive day she was not performing by herself: a small boy, who was a little like her, only with golden hair, came out with her onto the stage.

It was her brother. Yet once he had been Tutti the Heir.

The town was noisy, flags were flapping, wet roses were raining down from the flower-girls' bowls, horses adorned with plumes of various colours were prancing, carousels were careering around, but in Star Circus the little spectators were transfixed as they followed the performance.

Then Suok and Tutti were showered with flowers. The children surrounded them.

Suok took a little board from the pocket of her new dress and read something out loud to the children.

Our readers remember this board. One terrifying night, a mysterious dying man who looked like a wolf had handed the board to her from a sad cage in the menagerie.

This is what was written on it:

There were two of you: sister and brother – Suok and Tutti. When you were both four years old, you were carried off from your home by the Three Fat Men's guardsmen. I am Toob, a scientist. I was brought to the palace. I was shown little Suok and Tutti. This is what the Three Fat Men said: 'You see the little girl? Make a doll that's identical to that little girl.' I didn't know why it had to be done, but I made such a doll. I was a great scientist. The doll was supposed to grow like a living girl. Suok would reach five, and the doll would too, Suok would become a grown-up, pretty and sad girl, and the doll would be the same. I made that doll. Then you were separated. Tutti remained in the palace with the doll, and Suok was given to a roving circus in exchange for a rare kind of parrot with a long red beard. The Three Fat Men ordered me: 'Take out the boy's heart and make him an iron one.' I refused. I said that you mustn't deprive a human being of his human heart; that no heart – not one of iron, nor one of ice, nor one of gold – can be given to a human being in place of a simple, genuine, human heart. I was put into a cage. And from then on, they began to instil in the boy the idea that he had an iron heart. He was supposed to believe it and to be cruel and stern. I've been kept among the animals for eight years. I've grown a hairy coat, and my teeth have become long and yellow, but I haven't forgotten the two of you. I beg your forgiveness. We have all been deprived by the Three Fat Men, oppressed by the rich and the greedy gluttons. Forgive me, Tutti, which in the language of the deprived means 'One separated'. Forgive me, Suok, which means 'The whole of life'…

Biographical note

Yuri Karlovich Olesha was born on 3 March 1899 in Eliza-vergrad, the son of a former landowner. He moved to Odessa along with his family in 1902 and later studied law at the Imperial Novorossiya University until 1918. In 1919, against his parents' advice, Olesha joined the Red Army and served as a telephonist in a naval artillery base near the Black Sea.

Later, following his marriage to Olga Gustavovna Suok, Olesha would work variously as a propagandist at the Bureau of Ukrainian Publications in Kharkov, and later as a staff member of the railway journal *The Siren* for which he wrote satirical verse. His first story, 'Angel', was published in 1922, and was followed by two collections of poetry, and his second novel *Envy* which was published to mixed critical reaction in 1927.

However, Soviet policy towards writers became gradually more severe and the ambiguous message behind several of Olesha's works was seen as unacceptable, since it differed from the prescribed mould of Socialist Realism. Fearing arrest, Olesha ceased writing, limiting himself to translations and screenplays. *Envy* was condemned as reactionary and Olesha himself accused of 'antihumanism'.

The Second World War saw Olesha evacuated, along with the Odessa Film Studio, to Ashkhabad in Turkmenistan.

In 1956, three years after Stalin's death, a selection of Olesha's short stories was published. However, although the rules surrounding literature were gradually to be relaxed, Olesha died in 1960 before the literary climate was fully restored. His diaries were published posthumously in 1965 under the title *Not a Day Without a Line*.

Hugh Aplin studied Russian at the University of East Anglia and Voronezh State University, and worked at the Universities of Leeds and St Andrews before taking up his current post as Head of Russian at Westminster School, London. His previous translations include Anton Chekhov's *The Story of a Nobody*, Nikolai Gogol's *The Squabble*, Fyodor Dostoevsky's *Poor People*, Leo Tolstoy's *Hadji Murat*, Ivan Turgenev's *Faust*, Mikhail Bulgakov's *The Fatal Eggs*, Yevgeny Zamyatin's *We* and M. Ageyev's *A Romance with Cocaine,* all published by Hesperus Press.